AL CAPSELLA
AND THE WATCHDOGS

JUDITH CLARKE was born and educated in Sydney and now lives in Melbourne with her husband and son. She has worked as a teacher, librarian and lecturer, and has also published novels for younger readers and short stories and poetry in magazines. Her Al Capsella novels were first published in Australia and subsequently in America.

THE FIRST BOOK in the Al Capsella series, *The Heroic Life of Al Capsella* was included in the American Library Association Best Books for Young Adults list (1990), and was shortlisted for the NSW Premier's Literary Awards (1988). *Al Capsella and the Watchdogs* was shortlisted for the same award in 1990, and won the Variety Club Young People's Talking Book of the Year Award (1990).

Al Capsella
and the Watchdogs

Judith Clarke

THE O'BRIEN PRESS
DUBLIN

This edition first published in Ireland 1994 by
The O'Brien Press Ltd., 20 Victoria Road, Dublin 6.
First published 1990 by University of Queensland Press, Box 42,
St Lucia, Queensland 4067, Australia. Reprinted 1992.

Judith Clarke © 1990

British Library Cataloguing-in-publication Data
Clarke, Judith
Al Capsella and the Watchdogs
I. Title
823 [J]

ISBN 0-86278-311-9

10   9   8   7   6   5   4   3   2   1

Cover design: Christopher McVinish
Cover illustration: Cynthia Breusch
Printing: Cox and Wyman, Reading

Contents

1

Saturday Night

"What do you think?" I asked, whisking the soaked straggly lock out of the suds and holding it up under the scholar's lamp that my father, Mr Capsella, had bought for my birthday.

Lou craned forward, narrowing his small blue eyes.

"Does it look paler to you?"

"Darker, actually."

"That's because it's wet."

We were doing a bit of a dye test on a lock of Mrs Pine's hair, which Lou had quietly snipped off while his mother was taking a nap. It may sound like an odd way to spend an evening, but time hangs heavy on a Saturday night when it's raining and you've run out of money (we had two bucks seventy-five between us) and there isn't a party on anywhere because nobody's parents are going away for the weekend. A boring Saturday night could seem endless.

Yet in some other peculiar way, now Lou and I were pushing sixteen, time was speeded-up and scary: it seemed no more than six months since we'd started High School as ratty little Year Sevens, only a few years back since we'd all been finger-painting down in Never Never Land, Mrs Drago's kindergarten. Only eighteen months more and school would be over for good — the day you dreamed of back in Grade One and all the grades that followed after: that day when you walked into the Vice-Principal's office to pick up your exit papers. Now that dream had a tinge of nightmare round the edges; I didn't want to think about it.

Lou was given to little panics about things which wouldn't bother most kids, and he worked these panics up a bit, browsing through the horror pages in the local newspaper. At the moment he was obsessed by a snippet he'd read about a woman who'd chopped her tongue off, licking the cream from an electric egg-beater she'd forgotten to switch off. He'd hidden his mother's machine in the back of the garage, under a pile of old cardboard boxes, even though it meant Mrs Pine couldn't make pavlovas any more. And the idea of having a white-haired mother really freaked him out: I guess it made him feel old. I don't know why he didn't just ask Mrs Pine if she had a dye job — I'd certainly have asked Mrs Capsella. But then, I knew she didn't: no chemical firm would make a dye that colour, there'd be no market for it. Old Kelp, I called the shade, a grim beige tone like the bundles of dried-out seaweed you find along the high-tide mark.

I had worries myself, but they were ordinary ones: Year Eleven exams and Higher School Certificate looming on the horizon, and after that a sheer drop into space because I hadn't a clue what I wanted to be. Then there was Garnet Disher, this girl who was after me . . .

Someone knocked at the door, and a split second later, before I had time to say "Come in," or to shove the bowl of soapy water under the bed, my mother, Mrs Capsella, poked her head inside the room. She had absolutely no respect: we could have been trying on clothes or something.

"What are you kids doing?" she inquired, peering all

round the room and taking in the bowl and the ratty lock of Mrs Pine's hair which I still held between the tweezers.

"Just a bit of an experiment, Mrs Capsella," Lou answered brightly. He held his breath and wheezed cunningly hoping to distract her attention, hoping she'd ask if his asthma was coming on and whether he had his Ventolin with him.

But Mrs Capsella wasn't so easily taken in these days; Lou, like the rest of us, had lost his infant charm. She gave him a straight look which really did make him wheeze a bit and asked coolly, "What kind of experiment might that be, Louis?"

"Chem," I informed her smoothly. "We have to test these fibres for chemical contamination, and then write out a report." I nodded towards some papers scattered on the desk — luckily she was pretty short-sighted and wouldn't notice they were quite blank; fresh sheets I'd taken out of my folder for the weekend's homework. For years and years I've had this fantasy of doing all my homework first thing on a Friday afternoon: it's a dream I've never been able to turn into reality.

"Oh, sorry I interrupted," Mrs Capsella said, in quite a different tone of voice; you might almost say it was respectful. "Next time I'll knock."

"You did."

"What?"

"You did knock, you always do. But then you don't wait, you just burst in; we never get any privacy. If it was an adult in here, one of *your* friends, you wouldn't come in till they said."

"As if one of my friends would want to live in this rat's nest! By the way, did you know the phone was off the hook?"

"Is it?" I crossed my fingers. I'd been expecting a call

from Garnet; she'd caught me in the playground and made me promise to ring her on Saturday night. I hadn't exactly got round to it, and any moment . . .

"I've put it back again." She closed the door, and we listened to her Dr Scholl sandals clacking down the hall: they were the wrong size, that was one of the problems of buying your gear in Op Shops.

"You'll never guess" — her loud ringing voice came back to us, apparently addressing Mr Capsella — "they were actually doing homework! Imagine! Homework on a Saturday night; they must be getting serious at last!"

Serious! Lou and I exchanged glances.

"Let's get out of here," I hissed, thinking uneasily of the phone. "Let's take a walk round the old neighbourhood, check out if there's anything going on."

"In a place like Laburnum?"

"It's better than hanging round in a house where there's no privacy!"

"Right!"

We sneaked down the hall, holding our breaths as we passed the Capsellas' room. It wasn't late at all, just a little after ten thirty, but time is relative when you're hung over by parents.

". . . something in a bowl," Mrs Capsella was going on. "Water, I think, and some kind of greasy brown fibres —"

I wished she'd shut up; any moment my father would wander out to offer his assistance. His interest in schoolwork bordered on the unhealthy.

The front door was open, which was lucky, because it squeaked a little, but outside on the terrace Lou stumbled over the potted plants Mrs Capsella was growing for her friend Dasher, who was starting up a little business in herbal cosmetics. A window shot open and my mother's kelp-coloured head appeared.

"Where are you two going? Are you off to a party?" Her voice trembled slightly on that last word.

"A party!" I replied scornfully. "There's nothing on tonight, Mum, otherwise we wouldn't be stuck at home doing . . . schoolwork. We're just off on the prowl."

"The prowl?"

"Going for a walk."

"But it's the middle of the night!"

"It's only ten thirty. It's not even the beginning of the night, not for real people."

"Where are you walking to?"

"Nowhere. Just around."

"Well, watch out. There are all kinds of funny people about, you know."

"I can't see any." I nodded towards the empty street.

"You know what I mean," she said mysteriously. "Just be careful."

"Gosh, Mum, we can look after ourselves, we're nearly sixteen, you know, not little kids in prep. As if any —"

"Just be careful," she repeated, sliding the window shut.

"Hey, Mum!"

"Yes?"

"Listen, if anyone rings, I mean, if this girl rings, don't tell her I've gone out with Lou, just say I had to go to the doctor."

"The doctor? What'll I say was wrong with you?"

"Just tell her I sprained my ankle slightly, nothing serious."

"Can't I tell her something a bit less suspicious?"

"Look — just say I had to go to the doctor's," I snapped. In some calm, rational part of my brain, which didn't seem to function under stress, I knew she was right, but the thought of Garnet put me into such a panic that I seized on the kind of excuse I'd have given when I was eight years old and some nerd wanted me to go to his birthday party.

"All right, it's your funeral," Mrs Capsella grinned.

As we reached the gate she called after us, "When will you be back?"

"Not too late."

"Eleven o'clock? Eleven thirty? Twelve?"

"The speaking clock," giggled Lou, and I gave him a bit of a shove.

"Not too late," I repeated. "We'll be okay, Mum. No worries."

"Twelve? Be back by twelve."

We didn't reply. A statement like that didn't really rate an answer and we drifted on up the road, pretending we hadn't heard.

2

The Old Neighbourhood

It was really quiet around the old neighbourhood. Dead. We might have been walking through a suburb hit by a neutron bomb: the houses untouched, the people inside zapped into ashy dust. They were just asleep, I knew that; every adult in Laburnum seemed to be in bed by ten thirty, a fact I found almost as terrifying as the bomb — worse, perhaps, because it was voluntary. We passed Lou's house. There was a light burning there all right; Mrs Pine was waiting up for him. Another good Watchdog, just like Mrs Capsella.

I paused in front of the Bispins' place for a moment. Even at night, even in the rain, their garden was beautiful with its grassy sloping terraces and big shady old trees and I thought how I'd like to have a garden like that some day, even make one, lay it out piece by piece and watch it grow. Yes, that was something worth doing.

"Come on," Lou urged. "Let's take a look at Tatts Logan's joint; he's probably left the curtains open again."

Tatts Logan was a bit of a sad case. A few years back he'd been the local hoon, or lout, to use the old-fashioned adult expression. I could remember him trying to run me over on his dragster; he was still trying, though now he did it in his EH Holden. Tatts had taken early retirement from the school system, and afterwards he'd worked on the roads for a few happy years, wearing the old blue singlet and tattered stubbies, his big muscled arms printed gloriously with tattoos. But then he'd married Sharon Guppy, and Mr Guppy had found him an office job, and now Tatts wore a suit and a long-sleeved shirt, even in summer. At the weekends he mowed his lawns and cleaned his gutterings just like all the other married men in Laburnum, though he always had this weird dazed expression on his face, as if he couldn't quite credit the turn his life had taken.

Sure enough, the curtains were wide open at Tatts's joint, and through the window we could see Jacinta and Jason, the three-year-old twins, busy and happy with something on the floor. Those kids were the image of their father, except for the tattoos, and they were so over-active they hardly went to sleep at all. Lately, the Logans had hit on a new trick to deal with the insomnia problem; I'd heard Sharon telling Mr Glix all about it when she was buying gripe-water at the milk-bar. (I often wondered who drank all that gripe-water: Jacinta and Jason were far too old to have colic.) The insomnia trick went like this: at seven thirty Sharon and Tatts would tuck the twins up and tell them Mummy and Daddy were going to bed as well, then they'd go to their own room, put the light out, and pretend to be asleep. They reckoned the kids would think it was late, round midnight, which was their usual retiring hour, and drop off to sleep. But it was the Logans who dropped off while the kids stayed awake.

"What're they up to?" puzzled Lou. "They're all white and dusty-looking."

"Looks like they've been in the flour."

Although Tatts was basically a pie-and-chips man,

Sharon was a health food addict, and bought things wholesale: two big bins of stoneground flour had been tipped over the floor, and the kids were busy with their buckets and spades.

"We'd better wake the Logans up," grinned Lou. "Alert them, so to speak."

"Are you crazy? Wake Tatts up? He'll kill us."

"But the kids might get hold of the electric egg-beater. Or find their way into the Ratsak."

"Sharon wouldn't leave Ratsak where the twins could get it."

"Tatts might." Lou had a point there, and he hurried off down the side path, eager as a boy scout on Bob-a-Job day. I followed more slowly; I had a feeling this particular job might turn out to be dangerous.

It did. A few taps on the bedroom window and a big spotlight flashed on over our heads, the blind shot up, and Tatts's enormous head appeared behind the glass. Lou leapt behind the shelter of a big green garbage bin.

"Bloody kids!" yelled Tatts. "What ya think you're doing?"

"The twins —" I began nervously, but he wasn't in a mood to listen.

"Think you're funny, don't you, Capsella?" he bawled. "Creepin' round the neighbourhood, tapping at windows, scaring women in their beds."

"We only came to tell you that the kids —"

"Piss off! Get out of here, *pronto*, or I'll go right round there and tell your old man. Bloody little pervert!" He squinted sideways through the glass. "And you too, Pine, don't think I can't see you behind that bin!" His beefy arms, resting on the sill, were still as firmly muscled as ever, despite the office work. We didn't hang about.

"Serve him right if the kids swallowed the Harpic,"

grumbled Lou. "You know, if we'd been a few years younger, he'd have thought we were cute, waking him up like that, he'd probably have asked us in to supper."

"Not Tatts Logan."

"Maybe not him, but any other bloke. Now when we tap on a window, just because we're older and big-looking, people think we're perverts. Like Mrs Boland up at the fish-and-chip shop; she used to be so nice, she'd give us free potato cakes, remember?"

"Yeah."

"And now if we hang around in front of the shop she asks us to move along because we make the customers nervous. She doesn't even *recognise* us!"

"Yeah." There didn't seem much to say; I'd had a bad experience myself, just the Sunday before. I'd been sitting on the playground swings, mulling over a few small worries, when this woman with a little kid in tow had strolled over and ordered me off; she'd said I was too big for the equipment. It hurt, somehow.

"What'll we do now?" I asked as we turned the corner by Glix's milk-bar, a depressing dump with a gigantic neon ice-cream cone perched like a crashed rocket on the roof. The neon didn't work any more, nothing in Glix's shop worked very well, including Mr Glix. A while back, Lou and I had this daydream of running a milk-bar when we left school; it had seemed like the ideal job, nice and simple, lots of people to talk to, no qualifications needed. But the thought of Glix had put us off completely. He was an all-time loser.

Lou was staring at the metal ice-cream cone, transfixed. "Geez, that thing's depressing," he muttered.

"Snap out of it! What do you want to do? Go back home?"

He shook his head. "Let's go round to James's place for a bit."

"He might be working," I said uneasily.

Although James was almost the same age as us, he was already in Year Twelve; his parents had taken him out of our school in Year Ten — they said there was too much social life going on there, particularly in class. James went to this high-pressure school where you had to read two books a week: it didn't sound a big hassle to me, but it seemed to prey on his mind. He was always counting: counting the books and the pages in the books and the words on the pages. He claimed he'd read ten million words in two years and couldn't remember what any of them said, and he vowed that when he got out of school he'd never read anything again, not even a jam-jar label.

"If he was working," said Lou, "he's probably finished by now. No one works past eleven o'clock, do they? Even people doing HSC." He sounded frightened.

Mrs Cadigorn wasn't pleased to see us; she'd lost all her friendly ways since James hit Year Twelve. These days she only opened the door a crack, and when she saw it was us, she'd start to shut it again, as if we were a couple of religious maniacs out flogging tracts.

"Uh — is James in?" I asked.

"James?" Her voice went high and squeaky. "But isn't he with *you*? He told me that was where he was going. He's supposed to be working on his English Option, it's due in on Monday, and he said he was just going round to your place to get a breath of fresh air, he said he *needed to breathe*. Breathe! He never does anything else but — breathe." She passed a hand over her eyes, and Lou and I, frozen on the doorstep, exchanged glances. Mrs Cadigorn had the worst case of tunnel vision we'd ever seen, it was as though she was doing the exams instead of James. "Where do you think

11

he could be?'' she went on, taking her hand from her eyes and staring straight at us, pop-eyed with some weird kind of fright.

"He's all right,'' I assured her. "Lou and I went out for a bit of a walk, so —''

"You kids are always *walking!* Walking about in the night — why is that?'' She didn't wait for an answer, but went rushing on like a busted fire hydrant. "I'm sure he hasn't even *read* those English books. He said he had but when I asked him what Jenny's favourite film was —''

"Jenny?''

"She's a character in *Homesick Restaurant*,'' explained Mrs Cadigorn impatiently. "When I asked him the name of the film, and what its significance was in terms of the novel's theme, he didn't know what I was talking about.''

"Probably slipped his mind,'' I suggested. "He reads such a lot.''

"Does he?'' Her voice became eager. "I never really know what he's doing in his room, he could be studying, but then —'' she jerked her head queerly "— he could be just listening to his Walkman. He won't let me in, you see, he's nailed a little bolt on the inside of the door. Do you really think he reads?''

Louis shuffled his feet on the porch, he had this really basic, dangerous streak of honesty.

"Sure,'' I mumbled.

I used to think that Mrs Cadigorn was a calm sort of mother, the type who left you alone and didn't hassle. It was surprising what HSC did to people, parents especially.

"But where *is* he?'' she wailed, following us out to the gate and peering up and down the street.

"He'll just be round at Al's place,'' answered Lou,

his streak of honesty suddenly burning out. "He'll be watching TV with the Capsellas."

As if James would do that! As if any of our friends would risk getting caught alone with the Capsellas, or anyone else's parents, for that matter. We'd worked out a set of signals for my place: Lou and James never knocked on the door, they knocked on the window of my room, and I always left the living-room curtains a bit ajar, so they could check out the joint without alerting the Capsellas.

"No worries, Mrs Cadigorn," I said briskly.

She gazed at me with frank dislike. "Tell him to come back home before twelve o'clock. He needs a good night's sleep if he's going to finish that Option tomorrow."

"Geez," muttered Lou, as we drifted on down the street. "What a Watchdog! I don't think I'll do HSC next year; it unhinges people. The whole family could end up in the bughouse."

"So what'll you do instead?"

"I'll defer, put it off for a bit, head off to Queensland like Broadside Williams. He'll give me a job at the Sheltering Palms."

Broadside Williams had once been Garnet Disher's boyfriend (hardly a day passed without me wishing he still held the position). But Broadside had left school, he was far off in sunny Queensland, running a motel at a little place called Whisky Bay. He'd been passing through, and finding himself short of notes, he'd taken a job as waiter at the local motel. The manager had quit a few days later and Broadside landed his job. Don't ask me how, things like that happened to Broadside all the time: he had confidence in himself, I guess, and he passed it on to other people, at least for a while.

"Yeah, I think I'll head off," murmured Lou.

I didn't say anything, but somehow I couldn't see Lou getting past the outer suburbs. I could remember him running away before, years back: he'd taken all his saved-up birthday money and filled the pockets of his parka with oranges because Mrs Pine was keen on vitamin C, but he hadn't got any farther than the end of the street. He'd sat hunched up beside the fence of the reserve for a couple of hours, worrying about his parents and the dog and what he'd do when the oranges and the money ran out, and then he'd gone home again. Mr and Mrs Pine didn't even know he'd run away. Of course he was only eight then, but somehow I knew it wouldn't be much different now. You had to face the fact: some kids were successful escapees and some weren't. Lou was definitely in the second category.

3

The Good Old Days

James was waiting for us just down the street, sheltering from the rain under the big gum tree beside the Bispins' front gate. He was smoking a cigarette in one of the weird holders he used to keep his fingers free from nicotine; it was a forked twig, he had a whole collection of them, and when he walked along the street his eyes were always darting along the ground, seeking out new ones.

"You been to my place?" I asked. "Your mum said that's where you were going —"

The mention of Mrs Cadigorn was a big mistake; James's head jerked and his thick black eyebrows vanished up into the bushy fringe of his hair. "When I get a place of my own," he muttered, snorting out a puff of smoke, "when I'm a man, and I've got a house that belongs to me, and a garden, and a shed, I'm never going to let her into it." He waved his arm violently, and the cigarette flew out of his hand and landed with a little hiss on the wet pavement. "She can beg and plead, she can go on about how nice she was to me when I was a baby, how she washed my nappies and crushed up carrots in the mouli grater so I wouldn't get stomach cramp, but she's *never* coming in."

We were silent, watching the little wisp of smoke curl-

15

ing sadly in the air. I remembered this pathetic yarn Mrs Capsella had told me a few months back when she'd caught a glimpse of my report card, some tale about how she'd done her back in, long ago in 1975, picking up my teddy bear from the floor every time I threw it out of the cot.

"Yeah," I muttered, bending down to retrieve the burning cigarette.

"Chuck it away," ordered James. "I'm giving up smoking anyway. I might need the money."

"Let's go round to my place for a bit." I reckoned it was safe enough now, Garnet wouldn't ring after eleven thirty.

We strolled on down the street. Though it was a cold, wet night, the yellow light from the street lamps and the shadows cast by the bushes made you think of summer evenings in the holidays and the way we all used to hang out, sitting in groups on the garden walls, talking on till dark. James's mind must have been running along the same lines, for when we reached my front gate he gazed dreamily over the garden and sighed. "Gee — remember when we used to sleep out in your front yard, the three of us, in that old tent of Dad's, the two-man one? And make a fire and cook sausages and marshmallows?"

"Yeah." No chance of a barbecue tonight, I thought. The rain was getting heavier, and so were we: the three of us would never get into a two-man tent again.

"Hey!" shrieked James. "Remember Herbie?"

Herbie was this pet hamster I'd had years ago, a dull kind of pet who'd done nothing much beyond eating lettuce leaves and the wood shavings on the bottom of his cage. He'd died of a heart attack, keeled over one morning when a passing dog had stuck his nose against the wire to get a closer look. We'd buried Herbie in the back yard, not because we'd liked him all that much, but so

16

we'd have a skeleton in a few years time; we were only kids then.

"Let's dig him up!" screamed James, racing down the driveway towards the shed, tugging at the door, kicking over a stack of old paint cans in his excitement. He was like that these days whenever he got out of the house and away from his books, like a kid who's stayed awake all Christmas Eve, willing himself not to touch the Christmas presents at the end of his bed until the sun came in through the windows. Lou and I found him a bit scary at times.

A light snapped on in the darkened house and then, mysteriously, went out again.

"Shut up!" I hissed. "You'll have the Watchdogs out! Get the torch, it's on the shelf in there."

"Got it!" James's long, gloomy face was alight with purpose. He waved the spade at us. "Come on!"

We followed him down the back, lagging a bit, pushing our way through the tangles of old geranium bushes, blackberries snagging at our jeans. James was already digging down by the back fence, hurling clods of earth and stones and bits of rubbish over his shoulder. "Right here, wasn't it?" he prompted us. "Right next to that rotten paling in the fence." He dug the spade in again, deeply, and I remembered uneasily how I'd read somewhere that madmen had enormous energy. The whole situation was weird . . . though I suppose when you thought about it, the idea of digging up an old pet wasn't any stranger than conducting a dye experiment on a lock of your mother's hair.

"Hey! I think I've found him!" He knelt down in the mud and drew out a small, mouldy cardboard box. I closed my eyes.

Lou nudged me. "No need to freak out, it's just a few old bones."

17

"I wasn't freaking out."

"Isn't he great!" James beamed at us. "Here —" he thrust the remains towards me.

"You can have it. Use him as a —" I almost said "paperweight", and stopped myself just in time: the word was loaded, James had far too many papers. "Keep it as a souvenir of the good old days."

Lights flashed on in the house above. "Al!" cried a familiar voice. "Is that you?"

Mrs Capsella stood at the back door, a tatty dufflecoat from her own good old days hunched over her nightie. She seemed a bit disturbed. Unnerved by the scene with Mrs Cadigorn, I wondered if she'd been slyly sifting through the contents of my schoolbag, leafing through my assignments and reading Mrs Slewt's comments on my English essay.

"No worries, Mrs Capsella," called James. "It's just us."

"No *worries*! You kids had me scared to death; I thought it was someone else down there."

"Like who?"

"Never mind. Come inside, quick!"

"What's up?"

"Shhh." She bustled us inside the house, locked the door and turned to us, her face scared and mysterious.

"Have you been in my schoolbag?" I mumbled.

"Schoolbag? What on earth are you talking about?"

"Oh, nothing. I just thought — you looked a bit worried."

"I *am* worried, but I don't see what your schoolbag has to do with it."

"Forget it, Mum. What's the problem?"

"Did you boys see anyone out there?"

"Nope."

"I think there was a prowler about."

18

"A prowler? Who told you that?"

"Was it Tatts Logan?" put in Lou. "If Tatts rang up and said we were prowlers, Mrs Capsella, he's got it all wrong. We were just trying to help him out. The twins . . ."

Mrs Capsella gazed at him in astonishment. "Tatts Logan? What's wrong with you kids tonight?" A new alarm sprang into her eyes. "Have you been out drinking somewhere? With Tatts Logan?"

"As if Tatts Logan would give *us* a drink! Unless it was rat poison. No, *you* said someone told you there was a prowler about, and we thought that someone might be Tatts Logan."

"No one told me anything. I heard the prowler myself, tapping on the window of your room."

"Hmmm. Did you get a look at him?"

"He was too quick, but I heard him going off round the side." She paused dramatically. "He had enormous feet."

"How do you know if you didn't see him?"

"I could tell from the way he walked, kind of slow and dragging, as if he was carrying some huge weight. And then I opened the window —"

"You shouldn't have done that, Mum. If it was a real prowler, I mean."

"Of course he was real, I wasn't imagining things, Al. And when I opened the window, guess what I found on the sill?"

"What?"

"A burning *cigarette*. Imagine! And that's not all — there was a forked stick, a horrid, sinister little twig, shaped like a Y. What do you think that means?"

"Y marks the spot. He's coming back later. — No, sorry, Mum, only joking. I wouldn't know what it meant," I added, glancing at James, who was frowning,

19

sliding his hand in his pocket, feeling for his cigarette holder.

"Perhaps the twig didn't belong with the cigarette, Mrs Capsella," Lou suggested innocently. "It might have been separate, it might have been there for ages, blown by the wind or something."

"Dropped by a passing bird," I grinned.

Mrs Capsella looked hurt. "All right," she said, affronted. "Don't believe me. I suppose the bird dropped the cigarette as well. It was a prowler, I'm sure of it: a heavy, big-footed man, a smoker, whose name begins with Y. Are you boys sure you didn't see anyone out in the garden?"

"Not a soul."

"What were you doing down the back with the spade?"

Lou blushed. "Just mucking about. We —"

"Any phone calls while we were out?" I interrupted.

"James's mother rang to find out if he was here. You'd better call her, James."

"She's not my mother." James loped off down the hallway.

"What does he mean?" Mrs Capsella frowned.

"Oh, nothing. — Ask if you can sleep over," I called after James.

"Mrs Cadigorn *is* his mother, you know. Does he think he's adopted? I can remember when she went off to the hospital, a few months before you were born, Al. She —"

I stemmed the flow. "Any calls for *me?*"

"A girl rang. Ruby, I think her name was."

"Garnet." Actually, Garnet's real name was Sophie, she'd changed it when Broadside Williams headed off to Queensland. I suppose she didn't want to be reminded of the girl she'd been when she went around with him.

Not that Broadside had run off and left her: he'd offered to take her along, but Mr and Mrs Disher hadn't seen fit, and Sophie/Garnet stayed behind.

"What did you tell her?" I asked Mrs Capsella. "Did you say I'd gone to the doctor's?"

"Of course not." She smiled smugly.

"Mum, you *know* what I told you to say if she rang. Can't you even give a simple telephone message?" Panic washed over me. "What did you tell her? Did you say I'd gone out?" If she'd said that, then Garnet might think I'd gone out with another girl, and she'd be mad at me. Already there were quite a few girls at school who were annoyed because they saw me talking to Garnet in the playground after school: *she* was talking to me, I had nothing to do with it, but they didn't know that. And if Mrs Capsella had said that I was hanging out round the neighbourhood with Lou and James, then Garnet would think I was a *kid*. But Mrs Capsella didn't use words like "hanging out" . . . suddenly an awful thought struck me.

"You didn't tell her I was out *playing*, did you?"

"Playing?"

"You know how when I'm not here, and someone comes to the door, you always tell them I'm 'out playing', as if I'm a little kid."

"Oh, *playing*. No, of course not. I said you'd gone to visit your grandmother. You know, like Little Red Riding Hood."

There was no reply to that. "Just keep out of my schoolbag," I warned her. "I've got all my papers in a certain order and if you fiddle about in there you'll muck everything up."

"Listen, I don't know what you're implying, but I can tell you now, Al Capsella, I've no intention of dipping my fingers into that pigs' trough you call a schoolbag!''

"Good."

"Good *night*."

I followed Lou down the hall and into my room and closed the door firmly. Her voice came through it. "Keep your window closed, boys, just in case the prowler comes back. And leave the door open, so you'll be able to breathe in there. I don't like the three of you squashed into that little room; you're too big, there can't possibly be enough oxygen in there."

There was no way I'd leave that door open. Mr Capsella had this habit of getting up in the middle of the night; he claimed that was the only time he could really concentrate on his work. But concentration seemed to make him lonely; if he saw my door ajar he'd come inside for conversation. And when he realised he had an audience he'd begin telling all those crummy kiddy jokes he'd found in this book my grandfather, Neddy Blount, had given me for my fifth birthday: *The Little Folks' Book of Humour*, it was called. I was far more afraid of Mr Capsella's jokes than I was of death by asphyxiation.

4

One Hundred and Sixteen Days to Countdown

"Would you believe it, I've got to be home by eight!" James thumped the old sleeping bag as if it was a swans-down replica of Mrs Cadigorn. *"And* we're not allowed to talk all night; I've got to be 'fresh for my work'. Now I'm not even allowed to *talk*."

I set the alarm for seven forty-five. There was no point in getting Mrs Cadigorn worked up. In her current state she was perfectly capable of coming down at five past eight on the dot and banging on the door.

"Geez, *he's* the one doing HSC, but we've got to wake up at the crack of dawn as well," grumbled Lou.

Luckily James didn't hear, he was mumbling to himself like some poor old derelict on a park bench. "One hundred and sixteen days to countdown," he muttered. "One hundred and sixteen days, nine hours and ten minutes. Scene: The School Hall, nine zero five, on the seventh of November. Action: A bell rings. James Cadigorn opens his eyes and stares at the first page of the HSC English paper. He freaks out . . ."

"Oh, shut up!" hissed Lou. "Stop driving yourself mad."

"You just wait till next year," replied James gloating-ly, "when I'm free and you two —"

I switched out the light and silence fell for a little

while. Then Lou sighed. "What do you think Broadside Williams is doing now?" he whispered.

"Out with some girl," I replied, and for the millionth time I wished I was Broadside, a person who suffered from no hang-ups or embarrassments.

"Nah," said Lou. "I'll bet he's holed up somewhere with a pack of real hoons, playing poker."

"And winning," I added.

"Shut up!" protested James. "I've got to get some sleep."

I was just drifting into some queer dream about a clock when I felt Lou tugging at my arm. *"What's that?"* he whispered.

"What?"

"That — that noise. Hear it?"

I listened. Sure enough, there was a faint sound from the window, the kind of sound Mrs Capsella would have described as sinister.

"Someone's knocking on the glass — it's that guy your mum was on about: the one with the big feet, whose name begins with Y!"

The sound came again, sharper now, as if the person outside was getting impatient. Behind it you could hear the rain pouring down, and somehow this made it even more creepy: no prowler in his right mind would conduct his business in rain like that; it would have to be someone completely insane. A psychotic.

James started awake. "Shit!" he exclaimed, hearing the steady tattoo upon the window-pane.

"There really *is* a prowler," I whispered. "I thought it was *you* Mum heard outside. I thought that Y-shaped stick was one of your cigarette holders."

"Of course it was, but I'm not outside now, am I?"

My hands crept to the edge of the curtain, but I

couldn't draw it back, I just didn't want to see who or what was on the other side.

"Hey!" breathed Lou. "I bet I know who it is!"

"Who?"

"Tatts Logan."

"Ye—ah," I whistled. "That's just the sort of thing he'd do, after Sharon had made him clean up the flour. He'd knock back a couple of Fosters and then come right round here to give us a fright." I wrenched the curtain aside. "Rack off, Tatts!" I yelled. "We know it's you."

But we were wrong. Standing out there in the wet was Lou's mother, Mrs Pine, rain pouring down her face like tears, hair straggled, a raincoat slung over the kind of appalling night garment my own mother might have worn. And there were big furry moccasins on her feet! They were a surprise to me, those moccs.

"Sorry to wake you up, Al," she whispered. "But is Louis in there?"

"Lou? Yeah, sure Mrs Pine. No worries. I thought he told you he was sleeping here."

"Well, he didn't," she said tearfully. "I've been all round the neighbourhood, then I thought he might have sneaked off into town to some disco, come back on the train and been bashed up. His body flung onto the tracks —" She shuddered. "They do that, you know."

"We never go in trains, Mrs Pine."

"Are you *sure* he's there? You're not just covering up for him, are you, Al?"

"Oh no, Mrs Pine. Do you want to talk to him?"

"No, no, no, I'll take your word for it." She wheezed a little. That struck me as interesting: when Lou was a kid he'd suffered from asthma, now he was a teenager he'd gotten over it and Mrs Pine had developed the disease instead. It was pitiful. "As long as you're quite sure hc's there," she murmured.

"Do you want to see something of his, Mrs Pine? A shoe or something?" I fished about on the floor, found one of Lou's Reebok runners and held it out to her. The thing was covered in mud, practically ruined: those shoes, I knew, had cost two hundred and fifty dollars and given Mr Cadigorn some weird kind of seizure — he was a bit of a miser. But Mrs Cadigorn gazed at the ruin joyfully. "Oh heavens! What a relief!"

"You'd better go home now," I advised her. "It's raining."

"Yes." She added in a whisper, "Don't tell Louis I was here, will you?"

"No worries." She padded off up the side path, her moccasins slapping in the wet.

Lou was sitting bolt upright in his sleeping bag. "Was she wearing her nightie?" he raged.

"Relax, she had a raincoat over it."

"And her moccs?"

"Yeah. Hey, I didn't know your mum was a Bogan."

"Look, she's no Bogan. I wish she was, she might get off my back. The moccs are just for housewear."

"She was pretty upset," I mumbled. "I suppose she forgot to take them off. How come you didn't tell her you were down here, sleeping over?"

"Well, that's *why*. I mean, if I'd been going out to a party or somewhere, I'd have told her — sort of — but I was only down here, just three doors away."

"But she didn't *know*."

"Yeah, but —"

"Don't they *get* you?" squeaked James. "The way they fuss and bother and check up all the time? My mum wears a jogging suit!"

"What do you mean?"

"When she's out checking up where I am. She doesn't want people to know she's a full-time Watchdog so she wears this tracking outfit and runs round the neighbourhood at night, pretending she's out getting fit."

"Oh," I murmured. I'd often noticed Mrs Cadigorn, and lots of other middle-aged women too — mothers, I guessed now — jogging round the streets late at night, especially at weekends. I'd thought they were getting fit, but it seemed they might all be out looking for teenagers.

"When I'm a parent I'm going to neglect my kids," promised James. "It's healthier."

There was a tap on the door.

"Come in," I said repressively. It was probably Mrs Capsella; she must have heard the flap of Mrs Pine's moccs and begun fretting that the prowler was back.

But it was Mr Capsella. He peered round the room and an expression of sheer delight beamed from his face as he took in James's and Lou's presence.

"What do snowmen dance at?" he asked.

"Rack off, Dad," I said sharply. "We're trying to sleep."

"A snow*ball!*"

As I slammed the door shut behind the humorist, Lou remarked, "You're really mean to your parents. Telling him to rack off like that."

"What about *you?* You let your poor mother run round the block in her nightie and moccs; she could catch pneumonia."

"Hey," called James. "Just now I had this dream: I was walking across the face of this giant clock, and the hands were on nine zero five and one of my feet was stuck beneath the hour hand, and I couldn't move. What do you think it means?"

"I've had that dream," cried Lou. "Only I'm not on the clock yet, I'm just standing beside it, waiting to —"

"*Shut up*," I grated. "Let's get some sleep."

5

One Big Hassle

James's tunnel vision had a side effect which irritated the
rest of us: he'd ring up late at night to give you a blow-
by-blow description of the latest symptom. A while back
I got a call from him at one o'clock in the morning: he
thought he was developing this disease he'd seen on
some TV horror documentary, the kind of program Lou
liked to watch. The disease was called aphasia, and if
you had it you kept forgetting simple words.

"My mum sent me down to the shops to get some
vegetables," he droned, "and you know what happened? I couldn't remember the word for carrots, it had
completely vanished from my mind. I had to say 'that
long orange vegetable with the point at the end'."

"You should have gone to the self-service. Anyway,
you can't have aphasia, it's a symptom of senile demen-
tia, you're too young."

"You can get it through brain damage."

"From smoking, you mean?"

"Of course not, smoking doesn't give you brain
damage, it's grog does that. But you can get it from an
accident, a blow to the head."

"You mean the Watchdog's been getting rough with
you?"

"Don't be a shithead! I said an *accident*."

"You've never had an accident."

"I was thinking about that just now, when I was trying to get to sleep. Remember that time we were lying on the oval, back in Grade Four and that big kid in Grade Six came up and kicked me in the head, and then said he'd mistaken it for a football?"

"Toby Blood? He's in Torana now. But listen, that was years back — *seven* years."

"The damage could have come on *slow*. You know, there's billions of brain cells, you could lose a lot before you noticed, then one day it would start to show up. My theory is —"

"Look, is carrot the only word you've misplaced?"

"Well, yes, so far. But as I said, it's kind of creeping —"

"Look, it's half-past one, and I've got a maths exam tomorrow. Ring me back when you've forgotten some more words. Fifty or sixty, maybe."

Life was one big hassle, and not just for James. In Year Eleven, if you crashed a subject at school, the teachers started acting like you were already lining up for the dole queue. I was crashing maths; my brain had seized up like the engine in an old FC Holden and there was no way I could remember, or even take in, the lengthy explanations poor old Mr Tweedie tried to give me after class. At the beginning of the year I was getting fifty per cent, but by the middle I'd drifted down to thirty per cent. Mr Tweedie took me aside and administered a couple of IQ tests: in one I was a genius and in another so educationally subnormal I could probably have been put away for life. These results upset Mr Tweedie. I could tell that by the way his hand automatically reached into his pocket as he glanced down at the figures, searching for the bottle of Executive Stress Soothers he always carried on his person.

He popped one in his mouth and went through the columns again, hoping he'd made some small mistake. He hadn't. He turned back to me, a sad smile on his face, trying to make the best of bad news. "I wouldn't worry about it if I were you, Al," he said kindly. "I suppose if we averaged the results you'd come out with something pretty near the norm." He nodded his head reassuringly. "Yes, I'd say you're pretty normal."

"Who's normal anyway?" A funny expression flickered in his eyes; as if I'd accused him. "I didn't mean you, Mr Tweedie," I said hastily.

"It's all right, Al," he sighed, his brown doggy eyes glazed with hurt, and he turned and wandered off along the corridor to the staff-room. He had a little desk to himself in the corner there, where he sat marking tests and working out maths problems, while the other teachers chattered and laughed and mucked about like a gang of Year Eights in a free period. He worked too hard, Mr Tweedie; he took his profession utterly seriously and I guessed it made him a bit of a mystery to his layabout companions. There was a time, back in Year Seven, when I could never have imagined I'd ever feel sorry for a teacher. But things had changed; I couldn't help but feel a twinge of sympathy sometimes. Like so many other things, it made me realise I was getting on in years.

The Capsellas weren't much help with the maths. Mrs Capsella confessed frankly that she'd never passed a maths test since Primary School, and blamed it on her teacher. "He was a monster," she said darkly. "He had a cane."

"You mean he hit you?"

"Oh no, not me. He wasn't allowed to hit girls, but if a girl talked in class he'd make her stand up, and then he'd shout, 'Pick a boy!' "

"Pick a boy?"

"Yes, you had to say some boy's name, and he'd cane him instead, and if you didn't give a name he'd pick one himself, and it would always be a boy you *liked*."

"What a dickhead!"

"He scared me off maths for life!" she exclaimed, and I couldn't help but observe a note of satisfaction in her voice. "But Mr Tweedie's not like that, is he?" she continued. "He doesn't scare you, he always seems so — so mild."

"I scare him," I told her.

"You've probably just got a mental block about maths. I could get Dasher to give you some hypnotherapy, if you like."

Dasher was a friend of my mother's, and it was difficult to believe, when you saw her rigged up in her mini skirt and fishnet stockings and long, dangly earrings that she was actually a trained psychologist with real degrees and diplomas. Mrs Capsella had once shown me a photograph of Dasher at the age of thirteen: wearing a tight black skirt and a very low-cut blouse, she was leaning against a lamp-post, hands on hips, pointing her bust towards the camera. She was at least six foot tall even then, and I couldn't imagine her sitting in a schoolroom, filling in exam papers. She wouldn't have fitted in the desk.

Dasher didn't practise her profession very often these days, she found it stressful. Though she took the odd case, just to keep her hand in, she preferred gentler occupations like the herbal cosmetics trade. I liked Dasher: she never asked you dumb questions about how you were doing in school or what you planned to do with yourself when you got out of it; somehow she made you feel that life wasn't so scary after all, but full of possibilities. All the same, I didn't want her hypnotising

32

me; I had this dread that I mightn't come out of the trance when she snapped her fingers.

"I don't think I'd make a good hypnotic subject," I said.

"Oh well, you'd better drop maths then," Mrs Capsella advised.

Mr Capsella took the matter more seriously; he said he'd coach me. I watched over his shoulder while he laboured over the exercises, filling sheet after sheet of paper. Even with part of my brain seized up I could see that he was doing it in some special queer way of his own; sure enough, when he came to the end and looked up the answers, he'd got things way out of line.

"It's wrong," he observed, his voice shot through with pure astonishment.

"Yeah, I thought it might be. Better luck next time, Dad."

He shook his head impatiently. "No, no, I don't mean *I'm* wrong — *they* are. The answer in the book is obviously a misprint. It couldn't possibly be right."

"Mmm."

"I'll write to the publishers about it, it's a scandal to print wrong answers in the back of a textbook. In the meantime" — he cleared his throat — "while the correspondence is in progress, so to speak, I'll get you a tutor from the university."

The prospect horrified me. "Not Casper Cooley," I begged. "Or Dr Miggs. I don't like Dr Miggs, there's something wrong with his forehead."

"His forehead?"

"It goes up and down by itself all the time." I shuddered.

"I can't say I've noticed."

"Well, you wouldn't, would you? You're used to him."

33

Mr Capsella was hurt, he didn't like to hear his academic workmates disparaged. "Anyway," he continued, "I didn't mean one of my colleagues, I'll get you a student from the mathematics department." He glanced at me and sighed. "A really bright one."

But the bright student didn't make me any brighter, and I think I depressed him, because after a few weeks he rang up and said he couldn't come any more and the reason he gave was that he was "on a low". I was on a low myself: in the next exam my mark had slid to three per cent, and I couldn't help feeling it was partly Mrs Capsella's fault. As I was leaving for the exam she'd followed me to the gate, hassling me, begging me not to worry.

"I'm not worried, Mum, you're the one who's worrying."

"Anyway, Al, listen — this will cheer you up. No matter how *grim* the paper looks when you turn it over, even if it seems like you don't know a single answer, you couldn't possibly do worse than I did in my last maths exam."

"What did you get?"

"Three."

You mean three percent — three out of a hundred?"

"That's right." She smiled smugly.

"Geez, you must have been really dumb — practically disabled."

A flicker of annoyance crossed her face. "Nothing of the sort. I've told you, Al, it's got nothing to do with intelligence, you can be quite intelligent and still fail maths. It's all psychological, I had a simple mental block, just like you've got."

She worried me, and I was right to be worried, for when the papers came back, I'd gotten the very same mark. It was almost as if she'd cast a spell on me.

"Change subjects," advised Mrs Slewt, who was the Year Eleven Coordinator. "What would you like to do? Politics? Ancient History? Computer Studies?"

I shook my head.

"What do you want to be?"

I shook my head again. How I hated that question; it was getting so bad that every time I found myself alone with an adult I started worrying in case they were going to come out with it.

"Have you no idea at all?"

"Uh, no."

Mrs Slewt frowned. "You want to think good and hard about this, Al, you and all your scatterbrained friends; it's the most important decision of your lives. By the time I was thirteen, I'd already decided that teaching was my career."

Geez, what a loser! I could imagine exactly the kind of kid she'd been; the kind who made her dollies sit up straight and pay attention.

"Have you been thinking about it at all? You're nearly sixteen, time doesn't stand still, you know."

All at once a picture of the Bispins' garden, green and peaceful, floated into my mind, as it sometimes did in a tight moment. Only this time it seemed to have meaning. "I'm thinking of being a gardener," I heard myself reply.

She was startled. I guessed the image flashing through her brain: not trees and flowers and grassy quiet spaces, but a Tatts Logan type hoon in cut-off shorts and singlet, driving a beat-up utility with an untidy mess of spades and forks and rusty lawnmowers hanging out the back. "That's a *trade!*" she bleated. "Do you think your parents would like you to go into a trade?"

"But it's not them, Mrs Slewt," I protested

reasonably. "I mean, *they're* not going to become tradesmen." (Some hope!)

"Have you discussed the matter with them?"

"I'll get round to it."

"I doubt they'll be enthusiastic about the idea. A gardener!" She shook her head. "Well, we don't have *gardening* at this school, I'm afraid. You'll have to do Human Development, it's all that's left on the list."

"But, Mrs Slewt, that's *Home Economics!* That's for girls, it's *cooking* and stuff."

Mrs Slewt gave me a frozen stare. The Human Development teacher, Ms Rock, was her friend. "Now look here, Al, you boys in Year Eleven are the most chauvinist lot I've ever come across. Human Development isn't 'just for girls', as you so elegantly put it."

"But Mrs Slewt — there's not a single boy in the class!"

"That's because you boys are so narrow-minded."

"I don't want to do cooking!"

"It's *not* cooking. The cooking was done back in Year Eight. Human Development is a Proper Academic Discipline, it's an amalgam of sociology, nutrition and applied psychology. I'll put you down for it, shall I?" She raised her pen.

"Well —"

"Or would you like to do woodwork?"

Woodwork! I thought of the grim shed down behind the boiler room: it was rough in there, you could get injured.

"No worries, Mrs Slewt." I sighed. "I'll do HD."

6

Human Development

"We have a stranger in our midst," Ms Rock announced at my first lesson, and she sat me right up front, as if she thought I might have trouble with my eyesight. I suspected she wasn't all that pleased to see me; she had a theory that girls were more intelligent than boys, and you couldn't argue with her, even if you were a girl, because she'd just primp her lips together and say forbiddingly, "I've done Research."

Ms Rock had a really severe classroom manner; she believed in getting straight down to business the moment the bell sounded; there were no attempts at friendliness, no cheery little remarks about the weather or the weekend football results. "Unit Three," she announced sternly, and everyone opened their textbooks and assumed wise expressions because you were supposed to have done the reading the night before.

I flipped through the pages: Unit Three was all about how women's lives had changed for the better; there was an account of a pioneer woman's dismal routine and then a brisk, jolly description of a modern lady's daily round. It was this second story which puzzled me, and I could see, from a glance about the room, that it was having a similar effect on the more intelligent members of the class.

This modern lady, whose name was Maisie Bligh, had all her kids rostered to do Home Duties, and as soon as they were out of the house, worn out before their day had begun, Maisie nipped off to the Learning Centre to take her fitness class. After a barbecue with the other ladies, she headed off across town to the Craft Institute, where she was currently at work on a patchwork quilt for her daughter's Twenty-first. The daughter was fourteen.

There were murmurs amongst the girls; it looked like a class discussion was hotting up, but when Ms Rock said, "Any comments?" the murmurs died away like a cool breeze at sunset. Ms Rock frowned. It was so quiet you could practically hear the skin on her forehead crinkling up. Emma Chipper, who was a bit of a nerve case, giggled suddenly.

"Yes, Emma?" prompted Ms Rock. "Do you have a contribution?"

Emma squirmed and turned red. "I didn't know it took seven years to make a patchwork quilt," she remarked wonderingly.

"Perhaps the pieces were very tiny," suggested Melissa Pole. "You know, like postage stamps. That could take a very long time."

"That's not the point, girls," Ms Rock broke in sharply. "Not the point at all. What I'm looking for is some comment on the lifestyles: how they differ, and what this means for the modern woman."

Cherry Clagg waved her hand. She was a big, solid, cheerful girl, with a brain like a brick. I rather admired Cherry. Being dim didn't bother her at all, she failed all her subjects regularly, but the coordinators always promoted her so she'd pass through school as quickly as possible. If they could have put her up two years they'd have done it, but they were afraid of the Education Department.

"Yes, Cherry?" said Ms Rock, sighing a little and sitting up straight in her chair, as if bracing herself for Cherry's contribution.

"One of the ladies — the old-fashioned one with the big pole in her hand — she's doing washing, and the modern lady's doing needlework."

Ms Rock didn't reply. Cherry's contributions had the same effect on teachers as calls for class discussion had on us: they produced uneasy silence.

"Ms Rock!" called Melissa.

"Yes?"

"This Maisie Bligh, the one who's got all her kids rostered — well, she just goes off and enjoys herself. She hasn't got a job or anything, I think she's just a wanker."

"Just a layabout," agreed Emma excitedly. "And *mean*. I don't think it's fair to make little kids do the washing-up before they go to school. It would be different if Maisie was a boilermaker or something, but she's just fooling around. I like the pioneer better — she's tough. Look at the size of that copper stick!"

"The point is, girls," began Ms Rock, and then faltered a bit, as if she'd forgotten it. "The, um, point is, that Maisie's doing what she *wants* to do, she's no longer bound by the old —"

"No she isn't," said Melissa firmly. "Maisie's doing what the kid wants, it's the daughter who wants the quilt. Fancy wanting a quilt for your Twenty-first, she must be a real nerd; it's like she's keeping a glory-box, like she's in a time warp or something."

"The book might be out of date," I suggested, glad to have found something sensible to contribute before Ms Rock noticed I wasn't saying anything. I glanced at the front of the text: it had been published this year. Luckily Ms Rock hadn't heard my remark after all.

"Some women — sorry, Ms Rock, I mean people — *like* washing," said Emma. "I've got this aunt, and she washes sheets in lavender water, and then she irons them. She loves it; she says there's nothing she likes more than a nice clean sheet."

Ms Rock brightened. "Well, that's conditioning, isn't it, Emma? Your aunt was brought up to think that she should spend hours of every day washing and ironing, and she's grown to think she likes it. Now what —"

Emma shook her head vehemently. "But Ms Rock, my mum, that's her sister; she was brought up in the same family, so she should have had the same conditioning, and she *hates* washing. She just takes it all to the launderette every Saturday and dumps it there, and this poor little man, an old-age pensioner, he puts it in the machine and takes it out and folds it up all nice and neat."

"I know that old man!" cried Cherry Clagg. "He lives on the corner of Silver Street, near the milk-bar — he's got this big plaster stork standing in his garden. I love that stork!"

Ms Rock was turning red all over her face and neck, and her forehead twitched, just once, not on and on like Dr Miggs's did, but it was scary all the same. I decided to make a better contribution fast, before she noticed my silence.

"Perhaps Emma's aunt just does like washing," I began, "like some women, um, people, enjoy making sponge cakes, er, and studying medicine. People can really like boring things: my grandfather is really interested in garden rubbish, he spends whole afternoons pulling twigs off bushes, and leaves off twigs, and wrapping them up in newspaper parcels to cheat the garbage man. He's got a whole system worked out — he's really crazy about it; perhaps Emma's aunt is like that, she's got a little system and —"

Ms Rock turned on me furiously. "Al Capsella, I'm not interested in your grandfather's leaf-picking systems, that isn't what this subject is *about*. It's not a gossip shop we're running here, Human Development is a serious aca aca aca" at last she shot it out — "academic discipline."

"Sorry," I apologised.

"Ms Rock!" called Irma Doone, shooting her hand up and waving it wildly like a kid in primary school. Irma was the school poet, and most of the time in class she sat in a daze, but occasionally something would attract her attention and then she'd get really excited.

"Yes, Irma." Ms Rock looked wary.

"All the women in this book have cows' names."

"What!"

"They've all got cows' names: Bessie and Rose, and Maisie and Daisy, and there's a Mabel back on page twenty-one."

"What's that go to do with the price of fish?" Ms Rock demanded testily, and there were smirks all over the classroom because there actually *was* a piece in the book on the price of fish: it was in *Planning Your Family Budget* in chapter two.

"Nothing," said Irma mildly. "I just thought it might be significant, I thought the author might have *meant* something by it."

"This isn't English Literature, Irma."

"Perhaps the writer's a dairy farmer," I whispered to Melissa, getting into the spirit of things.

Ms Rock glanced in my direction. "What's that, Al? Would you care to share your observations with the rest of us?"

41

I didn't have time to think up a lie. "Perhaps the author used to be a dairy farmer," I repeated.

"I'll thank you not to come into this class and make chauvinist remarks!"

"Sorry," I mumbled. "Dairy farmeress." Ms Rock turned red again. "D—Dairy person," I stuttered. I seemed to be always apologising in this class. Mr Tweedie and his unintelligible figures were beginning to seem less like a nightmare every moment.

Ms Rock advanced on my desk. "Now listen, Al Capsella. I was a bit doubtful when you first came into the class; you boys who flunk out of maths are all the same: work-shy. You think Human Development is a vego — a soft option, a bit of a joke. Well, I simply will not have you disrupting the class with smart-alec remarks. See me in the staff-room after school. Three thirty on the *dot*."

"But Ms Rock!"

"Otherwise, you can leave this class and do Woodwork."

"No worries Ms Rock, I'll be there."

Whispers and giggles broke out amongst the girls, but they weren't laughing at me. Their eyes were fixed on the row of high windows which faced the corridor. Framed in one of them was a mop of curly grey hair and a pair of bright, interested blue eyes; they belonged to Mossy Crocket, the history teacher. Mossy often occupied her free periods wandering past the classrooms, listening in to other people's lessons. She didn't eavesdrop out of spite, it was simply a case of friendly interest: Mossy liked to know what was going on in the school and Human Development was just the kind of subject which fascinated her; I suppose she found it full of human drama.

"Just a moment, class," muttered Ms Rock. She

strode to the door and shut it firmly, then wound the handle on the open window and twitched it tight. She waited, silently, until Mossy's grey head had passed along the row of windows and vanished out of sight.

Cherry Clagg beamed delightedly round the room. "Mossy Crocket's lovely, isn't she? She's my very favourite teacher! Her house is just down the road from ours, and when I was little —"

"Cherry!" called Ms Rock warningly, and Cherry was silenced.

"Ms Rock!" It was Irma again.

"Yes, Irma?"

"There's a lady in the back called Blossom."

Ms Rock shot a wild glance towards the back of the room, as if she expected to see a stranger standing there.

"At the back of the *book*, I mean," explained Irma. "On page 205. It says, 'Mrs Blossom Keenan, aged fifty-four, is worried about her family's diet . . .' "

7

Snickerdoodles

I was a trifle late for my appointment with Ms Rock. We'd had Mossy Crocket last period and she'd taken us on a nature walk down in Bellbird Reserve. The walk had nothing to do with Australian History, the subject she was teaching, but few of Mossy's lessons had. By the time I got back to school it was a quarter to four, fifteen minutes past bell-time.

The staff-room, at first, seemed deserted; once that bell had gone, the teachers didn't hang around. I couldn't blame them, the place was cheerless, drab olive-green walls and scuffed grey linoleum tiles, lit horribly by a single flickering fluorescent light. Then I noticed a slight movement in one corner: it was Mr Tweedie, hunched over a pile of exercise books. I thought it was just possible he didn't have a home to go to, or if he did, it wasn't a very nice one. He used to be married to the music teacher, but she had gone away. Once I'd seen a lady picking him up in a car after school. She had white hair and steel-rimmed glasses and I hoped, for his sake, that it was his mother.

"Hullo, Al," he said now, smiling timidly, and at the same time flinching away a little in his seat, hunching himself smaller. I didn't take this personally, it was his manner with people, he quivered like an anemone in a rock pool when a little kid pokes a stick at it. Ms Rock, on the other hand, was more like a stingray.

"Looking for someone?" asked Mr Tweedie.

"Ms Rock."

He jerked his head towards the door and I saw that Ms Rock's desk was just behind it; she was stuffing books and papers into a briefcase so stiff and sharp that it might have been starched by the pioneer lady in Unit Three.

"Ms Rock —"

She looked up, blank-faced.

"You wanted to see me," I reminded her, "in the staff-room after school. Sorry I'm late, but Mossy Crocket took us on a nature, I mean, a history walk."

"Oh." She'd obviously forgotten all about it: out of sight out of mind. I could have saved myself the trouble and skived off. She seemed embarrassed. "Yes, well, remember what I said. You boys that flunk out of maths" — across the room, Mr Tweedie's flinch was audible — "never take Human Development seriously. Any more disruption, any more smart remarks, and out you go."

"No worries, Ms Rock."

"Make sure you do the reading I've set. How are you getting on with the rest of your subjects?"

"Okay."

"*Okay?*"

"I mean, I haven't failed anything."

"See you don't. Tell me, do you have any serious-minded friends?"

"Well, yeah — there's Louis Pine —"

Her frown was so deep it was almost a shudder.

"And James Cadigorn," I said hastily. "You remember him, Ms Rock — he was in Year Eight Home Economics."

"Ah, yes." She spoke through thin lips. "The boy who substituted foam-rubber lamingtons at the Display of Work, the one who almost choked two parents."

"You can't blame *him*, Ms Rock. Those parents shouldn't have been so polite, they should have spat the things out, instead of trying to swallow them. Anyway, James has changed, Ms Rock. You wouldn't know him; he's dead serious now."

"I doubt that." She sighed. "I don't think you and I can be agreed on the exact meaning of the word 'serious'. I meant friends who take their schoolwork seriously, who have responsible attitudes, who study before an exam, for instance, or do an assignment a little earlier than the morning of the day it's due." She put her head on one side. "Let me see — what about Sophie Disher? Or 'Garnet', as she calls herself now."

I was horrified. Garnet? How did she know Garnet was after me? Had Garnet said something to her, maybe asked her advice? Had Ms Rock seen something? But what?

"Sophie's a responsible girl," she went on. "Despite that regrettable interlude with Broadside Williams."

"Sophie?" I repeated stupidly.

"Yes, *Sophie*. You're friendly with her, aren't you? I've noticed you talking to her in the playground after school."

Watchdogs! They were everywhere. "She talks to *me*," I protested.

Ms Rock smiled frostily. "So? She's not supposed to, is that it? A girl has to ask permission before she's allowed to speak to a boy?"

"Geez no, Ms Rock. I didn't mean that, I'm not a snob. It's just that —"

"You have a relationship, don't you?"

"A relationship?" The word was somehow terrifying.

"You're *friends?*"

"Yeah, sure."

"Then why don't you and Sophie get together, say on a Saturday afternoon, or one night a week, and study together? It often helps to have a companion."

"Uh —"

"Would you like me to mention it to her?"

"No! I mean, don't go to a lot of bother, Ms Rock, I'll mention it myself."

"Good. I think —"

"Ah, Ms Rock." King Arthur, the school headmaster, loomed in the doorway. Although he was a big man, even huge, he moved with uncanny quietness about the school, materialising silently in unlikely places, catching you off-guard.

"Mr Arthur!" squeaked Ms Rock. "I was just on my way home."

"I'm glad I caught you. I'd like to have a small word — don't think I'm putting pressure on you — about the menu and catering arrangements for the Parents' Banquet. Everything in order there?"

"Well, I've just —"

"I had a little brainwave last night, Ms Rock. As we have several exchange students this year, I thought we might risk something with an American flavour, Transpacific, so to speak. You know the kind of thing: pumpkin pie, corn chowder, snickerdoodles — think you could manage it?"

"Snickerdoodles?" echoed Ms Rock faintly.

King Arthur nodded. "Surely you're acquainted? It's an old New England recipe, basically. Our former Domestic Science lady, Miss Kidmaster, served up a batch once for the Mothers' Union. It was a great success, and she was kind enough to give the recipe to my wife: I could get Mrs Arthur to look it up and give you a tinkle, if you like."

Ms Rock nodded dumbly, and with an encouraging nod, King Arthur strode off soundlessly along the corridor. I watched him from the corner of my eye; there were some kids in school (the ones who attended Mossy Crocket's lunchtime talks on psychic phenomena) who thought King Arthur possessed the power of dematerialisation. They believed he wasn't human at all, but a creature from the infernal regions. As I watched, the Headmaster's steps faltered, he came to a halt, and I waited for him to vanish. Those kids were wrong, he vanished all right, but not in any fashion you could describe as supernatural. He pushed firmly at the door marked *Staff Gentlemen* and disappeared inside.

I turned back to Ms Rock. "Domestic Science!" she spat.

"What?"

"It hasn't been called that for decades! And I'm sick of doing the dirty work round here; writing out menus and organising the food for these useless school bunfights, just because I'm a Home Economics teacher!"

"Human Development," I murmured, but she didn't seem to hear me.

"And I'm sick of people thinking I cook and sew and haven't any brains — none of the parents ever bother to talk to me at Parent-Teacher meetings, they don't think Home Economics is important! They think I'm a dill, they think I spend my spare time cutting out recipes and sticking them in scrapbooks, I'm just a kind of servant, a slavey — that's it, a kitchen slavey!" Her voice collapsed in a kind of wail.

I'd have liked to say something encouraging, something about Human Developments being a proper academic discipline, but the wail frightened me, I had this terrible feeling she was about to cry. I couldn't face it: I couldn't bear to see a teacher cry. I glanced nervously across at Mr Tweedie; he was hunched so low at his desk that he resembled an old coat slung across the chair. No help there. I turned and fled down the corridor, pausing briefly at the main door, checking out the playground, the oval, the courtyard beside the incinerator where the Year Twelves kicked footballs in their study periods. There wasn't a soul in sight, and the emptiness of the place seemed like deliverance after all I'd been through: at least Garnet had given up waiting and gone on home.

8

A Bit Withdrawn

There's an odd thing about parents and the Capsellas are no exception: they nag you to study, but the moment you go into your room, take out a book, and close the door, they come and knock on it.

I'd just begun browsing through Unit Four of my Human Development textbook: *Adulthood: Relevant Managerial Behaviour* when Mrs Capsella's guilty tap sounded.

"Come in!" I bawled.

"Are you working?"

"I *was*."

"Oh, sorry."

For a moment, seeing her at a disadvantage, I had the idea of announcing my plan to go into landscape gardening. Some instinct warned me against it; for all her eccentricities I suspected Mrs Capsella had typical parental dreams for my career, I could imagine her lips moving drowsily in sleep: "My son the lawyer," they proudly said. No, I'd postpone the revelation for a while.

She lingered. "Al —" she began.

"Yeah?" Her tone made me immediately suspicious; there was a wheedling note in it, she'd been up to something she knew I wouldn't like.

"Are you going to a party or anything on Saturday night?"

"We don't have any homework this weekend — I mean, we do have some, but I've already done it in free periods."

"I didn't mean that, I wasn't checking up, I just wondered if there was anything on."

"Yeah — there's a party over at Macca's place."

"You don't need special invitations, do you?"

"Nah, all the kids know when there's a party on, so everyone just turns up." An unpleasant idea struck me. "But not parents," I added. "Parents can't come."

"I wouldn't dream of it, I'm not that hard up, Al. As if I'd want to go to a teenage party! No, I was just wondering if perhaps you could take Oswald along."

"Oswald? Oswald *Padkin?*" I couldn't believe what I was hearing. Oswald Padkin, the school genius, never went to parties. He never went anywhere.

"That's right."

"But Mum, Oswald never mucks around with the rest of us, he doesn't even like talking; he shakes all over if you even say one word to him."

"Yes, I know. That's just it. I was taking a little walk this afternoon and I saw Mrs Padkin in her garden. We got to talking about this and that, and you know, she's really worried about Oswald's social development."

That was news to me. Ever since I was little I could remember Mrs Padkin driving kids away from her front gate; the only person Oswald was allowed to play with was his cousin, a lad called Gabriel Toovey, who'd won the Junior Mastermind title on TV. You'd see them in the front garden on Sunday afternoons, silently tossing a big beach ball to each other. They looked like an illustration in a Grade One reader, except that they were ten years too old.

51

"I thought Mrs Padkin didn't approve of social development."

"She's changed her mind; she's just done this course on teenage parenting at the Learning Centre and it's made her quite anxious. She thinks Oswald might be a bit withdrawn."

"A bit!"

"Yes, I know what you mean. I told her about that case Dasher had once, that really brilliant physicist who got this idea in his head that he was really a coatstand."

"You must have put her mind at rest."

"Well, as I told her, Oswald's only young yet, and we thought that if he mixes in a bit, gets to know a few people, he might loosen up. Now come on, Al, you can take him along to one little party, can't you? Let him tag along with you and Louis, so he doesn't have to show up by himself. It's awful walking into a room full of people you don't know."

"But he *does* know them, Mum, he just doesn't talk to them."

"That's exactly the point. He *might*, if he starts to mingle. You'll ask him, won't you?"

To be frank, the idea didn't appeal to me at all. You never knew with a person like Oswald: the way he shook and shivered when you said "hullo" bothered me, his Brillo-pad hair actually seemed to bristle with nervous electricity. Broadside Williams used to claim he'd gotten a shock from telling an off joke to Oswald Padkin: he said he'd actually seen sparks flying from his hair, and he showed us all a yellow stain on his finger which he said was a scorch mark, though it looked like nicotine to me.

I saw Oz outside the lockers on Wednesday afternoon. He was getting his folders out: they were neat and shiny with just his name and subject written on the front, none of the usual graffiti. I noticed again how small he was, almost like a primary school kid. Of course he'd skipped a few grades because he was so brilliant and Mrs Padkin was so pushy, but even a fourteen-year-old shouldn't have been quite as small as that. It made you wonder — did too much brain work really stunt your growth, like my grandmother Pearly Blount said it did? Mrs Capsella said that was an old wives' tale, and Pearly was certainly an old wife, but I couldn't help thinking, when I considered Oswald Padkin, that there might just be something in it. Take the Capsellas: they read a lot and they were shortish, while the guys in the school football team, who didn't get all that much time to read, were tall. The most convincing case was poor old James: at the age of fourteen he'd been six foot four and growing every week; he'd been shit-scared of ending up eight foot tall, the kind of oddity mothers told their little kiddies not to stare at. But ever since he'd been sent to that high pressure school he'd ceased to grow, he was stuck fast at six foot four and a half.

When you thought about it, people always imagined geniuses to be small. To test this theory I'd looked up Albert Einstein in the school library, to check out how tall he was. There wasn't any mention of his height in the biography, I don't suppose the authors who write those books consider this kind of detail important, but there was a photograph of him standing in a group of other people, and they were at least a head taller. It was the kind of interesting question I might have discussed with a bright person like Oz, if he'd been more conversationally inclined.

I sidled up to him as he stood beside the lockers. I don't usually sidle, but given the shaky state of his nerves it seemed wise to approach cautiously; there was no point in scaring him straight off. I cleared my throat, a polite sort of noise, non-violent, a teacher might have made it, and teachers didn't worry Oswald. He jerked round, and his hair really did bristle; Broadside Williams might have been right about that electric shock.

"Hiya," I said.

"Oh, hi." He fiddled with his folders, dropping a couple of them. And something else, something heavy, clattered to the floor. You won't believe this, but he had a *pencil case*, a wooden one, with a Thomas the Tank Engine sticker on it! As I bent to help him our foreheads clashed with a bone-shaking crack.

"Ow! You all right, Oz?"

"Yes," he nodded dazedly, clutching the pencil case to his chest.

It wasn't a particularly good start, but I ploughed on anyway. "Coming to Macca's party on Saturday night? Your mother said you might." I lowered my voice, I felt a fool talking about mothers in a school corridor.

Oz made a kind of lopsided movement with his mouth: a smile, I guessed.

"Yeah," he muttered, surprising me completely; I'd expected him to take to his heels when I mentioned the word "party". Perhaps the blow on the head had settled his nerves.

"Meet you at eight," I said quickly, before he could change his mind. "At your joint, right?"

"Right," he agreed, and I made off fast, for out of the corner of my eye I'd just spotted Garnet coming down the corridor.

9

Student at Work

"Look at that!"

"Danger! Student at work!" hissed Lou.

Through the window, we could see James lying on his bed, a Y-shaped twig held delicately between his nicotine-free fingers, blowing a line of perfect little smoke rings towards the ceiling.

Lou tapped on the glass. The effect was electric. James leapt to his feet, thrust the twig and the cigarette beneath the bed, sprayed a few shots of air-freshener from a can on the bedside table, grabbed a book and sank back down on the bed. His lips moved. "Come in," he was saying, his eyes on the door.

"What a nerd! He thinks someone's at the *door*. His hearing must be packing up."

"Don't tell him that." I bashed on the window. "Hey, James — over here!"

His eyes swivelled in our direction, and this time he got up more slowly, retrieved the cigarette from beneath the bed, sauntered across the room and opened the window. "What's up?"

"Want to come to Macca's party?"

He sighed. "Nah, I've got work to do."

"We noticed you doing it."

"I was getting ready, relaxing a bit."

"You don't have to work on *Saturday night*, do you?"

James frowned. "Look, you guys, there's only eighty-five days to countdown. Didn't you see that ad in the paper the other day? 'Only Ninety Days till the Most Important Exam in Your Life'?"

"Must have missed it. But you're allowed out on Saturdays, aren't you?"

"Sure."

"Then why don't you want to come?"

"Listen, I think I'm developing agoraphobia, when I get to go out, I suddenly don't *want* to; it's as if I'm scared of open spaces."

"There won't be any open spaces at Macca's party, everyone's going, even Oz Padkin."

"No," said James in a cool, elderly voice. "I'll stay here."

"Please yourself." We began to walk away up the side path.

James stuck his head out of the window. "Hang on a minute, I want to ask you something! Do you think it's possible to *lose* intelligence?"

"How do you mean?"

"Well, look at it this way. When we were in old Grunter's class, back in Grade Three, I was doing fine at schoolwork, wasn't I?"

"Sure, we all were, even Cherry Clagg."

"Yeah, but I was in Lions, the top reading group, remember? You two were only in Tigers. I was reading *Tales of Mystery and Magic* when you two were still struggling through *Fay and Don at the Farm*."

"We weren't exactly *struggling*. Anyway, I *was* in Lions, only Grunter put me down for talking. Mum went up to the school about it, but they threw her out."

"I could have been in Lions," put in Lou. "But I

didn't like it: if you were in Lions you were always worrying about being put down into Tigers, but if you were in Tigers you had it easy. I mean, you couldn't possibly get put down into Elephants, Elephants was just Cherry and her alphabet cards.''

James shook his head impatiently. "Okay, okay, so you two were *really* Lions, you were just in Tigers because Al was talkative and Lou had an anxiety neurosis. But that isn't the point, what I'm saying is that I was intelligent then, and I don't feel intelligent now. So what happened? Can you get to be a moron, when you weren't one to start off with? Does ten years of school *do* something to you?''

"We had something like that in Human Development last week,'' I told him. "Prolonged exposure to a psychopathic environment can undermine even the most stable personality . . .''

"I'm not talking about psychopaths!''

"No, but it's the same process, you just change the word. Broadside Williams always said school was moronic, so prolonged exposure to a moronic environment could undermine even the sharpest intelligence —''

"Thanks a lot. When you guys are doing HSC I'll be round on Saturday nights, giving you a bit of encouragement, boosting your confidence.'' He slammed down the window.

"He makes me nervous,'' grumbled Lou, as we trudged up Pepperel Street towards the Padkins' place. "Do you really think he's got all those things he thinks he has: aphasia, agoraphobia, disintegrating brain cells?''

"Just a bad case of tunnel vision. It's all in the mind.''

"But brain cells *are*, aren't they? In the mind, I mean.''

57

"Shhh," I said, partly to shut him up, and partly to warn him. For we had reached the Padkins' front gate.

10

Science Fiction

And there we stalled. The simple fact was that we were scared of Mrs Padkin, we couldn't help recalling all those times she'd told us off for hanging round the gate or kicking our football in the street outside. They were long past now, but the memories lingered on.

"C'mon," I said, pushing at the well-oiled gate, but halfway up the path Lou grabbed at my new shirt. "Hey," he whispered. "Are you sure your mother got it right? That Mrs Padkin actually *wants* us to take Oz out?"

"That's what she said."

"Yeah, I know that's what she *said*, but you know what your mother's like, she gets everything mixed up — real people and the people she writes about. She might have thought up some story about Mrs Padkin getting worried about Oz's social development, then she forgot it was a story and thought it was real —"

I hesitated. He could be right: that kind of thing happened far too often with Mrs Capsella, who was a writer of the kind of wanky yarns that English teachers referred to frankly as trash. "But she told me all this detail about the conversation they had, it sounded really convincing."

"That's her job, isn't it? To make up convincing details."

Before we had time to think further, a light flashed on in the front room and we saw a long, stork-like shadow pass behind the curtains, heading purposefully for the front door. Lou began to back down the path.

"Don't skive off," I told him. "She's heard us out here anyway; she'll ring Mum, they'll track us down at the party."

"You talk to her then," urged Lou. "You make a better impression than me."

"How do you mean?"

"You just *look* better, you know how Mr Santini at the pizza shop said I was a funny-looking kid."

"That was years ago, you were *nine*, for God's sake, and anyway, he says that to just about everyone."

"But not as often as he said it to me. I *am* funny-looking."

"Get a hold of yourself, will you? Mrs Padkin's only someone's mother. And if she kicks us out, that's all right, because then we don't have to take a nerd like Oz along to the party."

But when Mrs Padkin opened the door, we got quite a shock — she was beaming all over with welcome; Mrs Capsella had got it right for once. "Hullo Al," she trilled, "and — and that's Louis Pine back there, isn't it? Hullo, Louis."

"Hullo, Mrs Padkin," he muttered.

"Come along in," she urged us. "Don't stand out there in the cold. You can't afford to take a chill at this time of year, can you?"

"This time of year?"

"Well, so very near the exams. Only seven and a half weeks to go, now."

"Oh, yeah."

"Stiff course, Year Eleven," rumbled Mr Padkin, creeping out from behind the coatstand.

"Coping, are you?" asked his wife, thrusting her long-chinned crocodile face towards us.

"Coping?"

"With your courses. Homework, assignments, that kind of thing."

"Sort of."

"Nice to get your teeth into some real work, though, isn't it? What subjects are you doing? Physics? Pure Maths? Chemistry?"

"Now, Pammie," admonished Mr Padkin. "Remember?"

"Oh yes." Mrs Padkin smiled and put a finger on her lips. "Naughty of me. I was forgetting, it's Saturday night and you boys don't want to hear about schoolwork on a Saturday night, do you?" She straightened her shoulders and smiled coyly at her husband. "Melvin and I were talking about that very subject when we heard you boys making a noise out on the path."

"What subject, Mrs Padkin?"

"Recreation. We believe there's a proper place in the senior years for rest and relaxation, don't we, Melvin?"

"All work and no play makes Jack a dull boy," intoned Mr Padkin.

"Yeah," agreed Lou brightly. "Boys and girls come out to play, the moon doth shine as bright as day."

The Padkins stared at him doubtfully, and Mr Padkin rubbed his hands together nervously. "Oswald's just down in his room, along the hall," he informed us. "Last door on the right."

"He's getting ready," added Mrs Padkin.

"Been at it all day," confided her husband proudly.

"He went off to Westfield this morning all by himself on the bus, to do a spot of shopping."

"Clothes," murmured Mrs Padkin.

Clothes! I'd been worrying about that all afternoon. For years, ever since primary school, Oz had been known as the Drip Dry Boy: in summer he wore drill shorts, long white socks and a neat white sports shirt; in the winter he favoured pullovers and long trousers, sharply creased, in a certain shade of spinach-green.

"He was laden down!" breathed Mr Padkin. "Boxes and bags all over the place."

"We didn't peep," added Mrs Padkin righteously.

"We believe teenagers have a right to their privacy."

I had a sinking feeling that those bags and boxes contained nothing more exciting than a new pair of green trousers and a lambswool sweater in a slightly more dashing shade than usual: powder-blue, perhaps, instead of college grey. Oz was certainly no sucker for high-pressure teenage advertising; fashion meant nothing to him, he could have strolled through a time warp back into the 1940s, and no one there would have raised an eyebrow.

You couldn't really miss Oz's room; there was one of those china plaques nailed to the door: *Oswald Sleeps Here*, it read, and there was a picture of a little kid nursing a puppy in his lap.

"Check that out, will you?" snorted Lou. He doubled up and then straightened back fast as a whisper sounded behind us. Forgetting all about teenage privacy, Mrs Padkin had followed us like any other mother. Walking on tiptoe, like a stork in point shoes, she beckoned us away from the door. "This party," she began. "Where is it, exactly?"

"At Macca's joint."

"Macca?"

"Andrew Mcleod. He's a kid in our year."

"Do I know him?" She put her head on one side, regarding me brightly.

"Probably you wouldn't, Mrs Padkin, he's only new. He got kicked out of — I mean, he's just changed schools."

"Oh. Where does he live, exactly?"

"Over Dartmoor Road way."

"In Dover Street? Afton Avenue?"

"Sort of Afton Avenue. Round the corner, down a bit, one of those little courts —"

Mrs Padkin tired of me and turned to Lou. "Do you know the exact address, Louis?"

"Pam," murmured Mr Padkin, tiptoeing up behind his wife. He put a finger to his lips and winked at her. "Privacy," he whispered.

"Yes, but what if something happens!" wailed Mrs Padkin in an odd, muffled kind of shriek.

"Nothing will happen," soothed Mr Padkin. "These boys are men of the world." Mrs Padkin glanced at us doubtfully as she allowed herself to be led away.

I knocked on Oswald's door. The plaque rattled against the wood, and Lou pulled it off the nail and slipped it into his pocket.

"What are you doing?"

"Shhh."

"The Padkins will think we're shoplifters or something!"

"So what? Hey!" His attention was caught by the next door down the hall; there were two plaques on it, side by side: *Cyril Sleeps Here*, and *Pammy Sleeps Here*. "Now check *these* out!"

"Lay off, will you? You'll have them back here." I knocked on Oz's door again.

"Come in," he called, in that curious voice of his, which was both deep and squeaky at the same time.

The room was in darkness except for the greeny glow of the cut-out stars pasted on the ceiling. I had stars like that in my room; they came in paper sheets and you pressed them out and stuck them on, and when you turned the light off at night it was like lying under a starry sky. But my stars were stuck on any old way; Oz's were arranged in real constellations, the Southern Cross and Orion, with Venus low down on the horizon. It looked great; there were advantages in being as well-informed as Oswald.

I sniffed suddenly; there was an odd, sharp smell of glue in the air. Lou and I exchanged glances. Oswald Padkin — a secret glue-sniffer! Only yesterday the very idea would have seemed like the sheerest fantasy, but seeing the Padkins close up had unnerved me; you'd need some sort of refuge if you had a pair of crocs like that around the house. Not one that gave you brain damage though. Brain damage! With some kids, a spot of the old BD mightn't make much difference, but with a brain like Oswald Padkin's the ill effects of glue sniffing would really count. He wasn't just a swot, he was brilliant, if he'd been a cave-man he would have discovered the wheel.

The light snapped on. We gasped. The room was amazingly tidy: the clothes were in the cupboard and the books were on the bookshelves, the top of the desk was clear and clean and ready for action, not scattered all over with chip packets and hair gel and photographs, like the desks of most of the kids I knew. There wasn't a single object on the carpet, not even a pair of shoes, you could walk straight across that floor without treading on anything! But it wasn't the neatness which surprised us — after all, you'd expect the owner of a pencil case to be

64

neat. It was the person on the bed. I knew it was Oswald, because he was so small, but there the resemblance ceased altogether. The boy on the bed glittered all over: his jeans and sweatshirt were covered so thickly with studs and sequins and glass beads that you couldn't see the material beneath, his socks were fluorescent, the sneakers sprayed with luminous paint.

But it was Oswald's hair which gave us the biggest shock. He'd shorn it off, almost shaved his head; there was just a narrow strip left along the centre, a kind of mohawk in a weird orange shade.

"Where'd you get *that* done?" breathed Lou. "Caro?" Caro was one of the girls who'd left school in Year Ten; she'd gone to work in The Peppercorn, a hairdressing establishment in the shopping centre. She was only a first-year apprentice, but she was making quite a name for herself, giving all the kids fancy cuts after hours, cut-price.

"I didn't have time to get round to Caro's," answered Oz coolly. "I did it myself, with the electric razor." He smiled proudly, and I noticed that he wasn't shaking like he usually did.

"Funny shade of dye," I remarked. "How'd you get such an even colour?"

Oz smiled mysteriously and I looked more closely: there was something strange about that hair, the texture — it was thick and woolly and stood up straight in a perfect, even ridge. I touched it; the stuff wasn't just woolly, it really *was* wool. "Carpet," I said faintly.

"Shagpile," agreed Oz. "There was a roll out in the shed, left over from the sitting-room. I glued it on with Airfix."

"Looks great," I mumbled.

"Smells great, too," remarked Lou, catching my eye.

Airfix! So that was it. Relieved, I flung open the win-

65

dow and a cold blast of air rushed in. We all breathed deeply and Oz's face began to take on its ordinary rose-pink flush. "I used it on the shirt and jeans as well," he said, indicating the spangles. "Stinks a bit, but it looks great, doesn't it?"

"You'll be the belle of the ball," Lou said cheerfully, but I noticed he cast a quick, fearful glance towards the door and I knew he was thinking, as I was, of the Padkins waiting outside to see their son in his new party clothes.

"Is there a back door?" I asked.

"There's the window," said Lou. "Let's go that way."

"Why do you want to use the window?" asked Oz. "This house has a front door."

"But your folks! Have they seen —"

"No worries," said Oz confidently. I'd never heard him use a phrase like this before. It was quite new to him, and he said it over to himself a few times, lingering-ly, a pleased expression on his face. "No worries," he repeated. "The folks have reformed. They've turned over a new leaf since Mum did that teenage parenting course." He ran a hand lightly over his mohawk. "Wait till they see!" I felt, with a sickening lurch deep down inside somewhere, that I could wait quite a while.

"C'mon!" Oz sprang from the bed and hustled us in-to the hall. It was deserted, and for a moment I thought the Padkins, mindful of our teenage privacy, might have retired discreetly to their bedroom. But just as we reach-ed the front door they appeared as magically as King Ar-thur looming up in the boys' locker room at recess. They gazed and gazed, and their eyes reminded me of the dogs in *The Tinder Box*: Mr Padkin's were as big as saucers, while Mrs Padkin's resembled the dog who sat on the box of silver, the one with eyes as big as mill-wheels.

66

"Who's that?" she asked, and her husband made a queer strangling sound in his throat. They were looking straight at Oswald, but it was clear they didn't recognise their son, they must have thought he was some kind of punk who'd sneaked in behind us.

"Hi folks!" squeaked Oz. He gave them a little wave with stiff fingers, touching his forehead in a kind of salute.

"Oswald!"

"Wonderful get-up, son," gasped Mr Padkin, getting control of himself fast. "I like the fringed skull-cap."

"Skull-cap! No way — it's real," boasted Oz, and he seized his mother's trembling fingers and ran them over his prickly skull.

She flinched away with a small whimpering sound. "He looks like an *alien*," she cried, tugging at her husband's jacket. "Doesn't he, Melvin — he looks just like something awful from Outer Space."

"It's okay, Mrs Padkin," said Lou comfortably. "Hair grows back in no time. There's this kid I know, Skull he calls himself, and he —"

"We'd better be going," I interrupted, "don't want to be late." Skull's story wasn't really all that suitable for Mrs Padkin's ears.

As we stood outside, getting ourselves together, I heard Mr Padkin gamely offering comfort to his wife. "It's exciting, dear," he was saying. "These are new horizons. It's like living in a science fiction novel, Pammie."

11

Pies

"Let's buy a pie," said Oz eagerly, as we turned the corner of Pepperel Street and Glix's milk-bar came into view.

"A pie?"

"Yeah, a meat pie. You know — Tubby Tom, Top n'Tail, Slurpmaster —" he reeled off a string of brand names, proud as a clever three-year-old mastering the alphabet.

"What do you want a pie for?"

"To eat, of course."

"I'm not hungry," I said. "The stink of that glue of yours was a meal in itself."

"Oh, come *on*," he urged. "I never get to eat pies, Mum thinks they're full of salmonella."

"Glix's probably are; he doesn't move his stock all that fast."

"It's pretty late," added Lou. "I don't think he'll be open."

"Glix is always around," persisted Oz. "He never goes out."

He was right about that. As we drew near the milk-bar Glix's stout form emerged from the shadows of the doorway; he was dragging a huge cardboard carton across the threshold. We gave him a hand.

"More bargains, Mr Glix?" asked Lou, nudging one of the boxes with his right foot. That was one of the odd things about Glix's shopkeeping; although he was frequently out of items like sugar or flour or plain old milk, he had a big supply of all kinds of junk that no one wanted, the sort of stuff you usually find in the bottom of cheap show-bags.

"Don't touch the stock," replied Glix nervously.

"Yeah, but what *is* it? Celluloid dollies? Rainbow pens? Find-the-missing-piece jigsaws?"

"Birthday cards," said Mr Glix proudly. "Got them dirt cheap, ten cents each, would you believe it? I can sell them for fifty, I'll make a big profit on this line, boys, no worries. There's four thousand in there. Four thousand times forty cents, that's sixteen hundred dollars!"

"Four thousand!" exclaimed Lou. "That's quite a stack, Mr Glix."

"They're quality items," Glix enthused. "No rubbish. Look!" He lifted the flap on the box and drew out a card. "Are your hands clean? I don't want fingerprints on the stock."

"We're going to a party, Mr Glix, of course we're clean. We're not grubby little kids, you know."

"Okay." Glix handed me a card. Above a large bouquet of shiny roses, a motto was picked out in gold. *"Happy Birthday on a Tuesday,"* I read. Lou, peering over my shoulder, snorted.

"First-rate stuff, eh?" said Glix, his eyes alight with pleasure. I couldn't disappoint him. "Great!" I said.

"Hey!" Oz spoke excitedly. "Mr Glix!" I nudged him but it had no effect.

"Yup?"

"Mr Glix, do you know that the mathematical odds against four thousand people with friends born on a

Tuesday, and absent-minded people, the ones who forget to buy their cards at the shopping centre and have to come to the milk-bar at the last moment —'' he paused for breath ''— four *thousand*, living in Laburnum, and a small area of Laburnum at that —''

This time I kicked him sharply on the ankle. "Ouch!" He bent to rub at his fluorescent sock.

"This guy wants a pie," I told Mr Glix hastily. "Any chance of one?"

Oz forgot all about mathematical probability. "That's right, Mr Glix," he cried. "I want a pie." He closed his eyes dreamily. "I think I'll have two."

Glix glanced at him with irritation. He hated to sell you the kind of dull stuff usually found in milk-bars. "Run out of pies," he muttered in a bored tone.

"No you haven't," persisted Oz. "I can see them there, in the fridge, those little square things in paper bags."

"They're cold. And the microwave's not working."

"No worries, Mr Glix: I'll have them cold."

It made Lou and me quite queasy, walking beside Oz, listening to him munch those cold soggy pies; it was like listening to a cat chewing a particularly slimy piece of ox liver. I kept sneaking glances in his direction; I couldn't get over the way he'd changed, almost overnight, into an entirely different person, like James when he went off to private school. Mrs Capsella had a book on her shelves called *The Shaking of the Foundations:* on the cover there was a picture of a tiny little man standing beneath a towering wall which was cracked and crumbled at its base. These days I often seemed to find myself in situations where that picture flashed into my mind.

"Great," Oz was murmuring between clammy mouthfuls. "Just great!" He paused under a street light to examine the paper wrapping. "Look — it's got a black crow on it. Why do you think that is?"

We didn't answer.

12

Down in Macca's Bungalow

Macca's house was one big crush; you couldn't move, and because of the smoke you couldn't even breathe very well. All the same, I was grateful for the crowd because Garnet was there on the other side of the room and I could tell by a certain jumpiness about her eyes that she'd been watching out for me. She waved, and I had to wave back, and then, of course, she began to move in my direction. She didn't get far; there were too many bodies and she couldn't find a path: when a space cleared for a moment she'd get a little way across and then she'd be swept back like some luckless surfer stranded by an unfriendly tide. I wasn't helping by edging back a little, inch by inch, like a receding shoreline.

It's weird how girls make you feel guilty when you haven't really done anything. I liked Garnet, but I'd liked her a lot more before Broadside Williams had gone off and she'd switched her attention to me. I was nervous; I couldn't help remembering how when she went with Broadside she always had these lovebites on her neck. I didn't really have a clue how to make lovebites, even though Broadside had given demonstrations in the playground.

"Hi, Al."

I jumped, but it was only Kelly Krake, and I was glad

to see her. Kelly was okay, you were safe with her, she just liked food. Once she'd been a thin girl who worried so much about being fat that she'd taken to compulsive eating; now she was plump and she found it didn't bother her, so she'd given up worrying about her looks and now she was free to concentrate on other things. She had a part-time job at Dizzy's Ice Cream Parlour and was saving money to go on a trip to India. Being fat was considered a mark of beauty there, she told everyone. Actually, she wasn't really fat at all, just slightly plump, and you only noticed that because most of the girls had figures like Mrs Padkin's, thin and stork-like, though their faces weren't quite so frightening.

"Hey, did you see Oz?" I asked.

She shook her head. "Unbelievable. I could hardly recognise him. What did his mum say?"

"Not all that much, she was in shock I think."

"Bet he's got to be home by twelve, like Cinderella."

"It's one, actually. We've got to take him home, too."

"Poor old Oz!"

"I can't get over how cool he is," I said. "He wasn't shaking a bit, he's generally scared stiff of people, and this is his first party."

"Must have got a crack on the head."

I stared at her, suddenly remembering how I'd bumped into him outside the lockers. "Do you really think so?"

"Only joking, it's probably just delayed puberty or something. Let's go into the kitchen, I want to get something to eat." She cleared an easy passage for us through the crush; she was more solid than Garnet, and more determined. Obviously she must be keener on food than Garnet was on me — there was some hope in that, I thought. After all, if Garnet was really interested, she'd have made it through the crowd no matter what. Perhaps I was worrying about nothing.

We grabbed a few sausage rolls and a couple of cans and squeezed into a narrow space between the stove and the refrigerator. It was a tight fit, but comfortable enough. I gazed round the room. Most of the kids at the party were familiar to me, a lot of them I'd known since Mrs Drago's kindergarten. Never Never Land! Lou and I often walked past the old place. The same old sandpit and swings were still there in the front garden with little kids yelling and tumbling all over them. We'd stop and watch them for a minute and every time, as we walked on past the plate-glass window of the shop next door and saw our reflections, long and gangly, staring out at us, we'd get a big shock. We'd think, "Who are those two blokes?" and get a scared, shrinking feeling when we realised they were us. "Hey, mister!" one of Mrs Drago's kids had yelled out once, and we'd looked behind us, but no one was there. "Hey, mister, rack off!" You wouldn't think a four-year-old would know a phrase like "rack off!" He must have had an older brother.

"What's the matter?" asked Kelly. "You look a bit bleak. Worried about the Padkin reception committee?"

"No. I was just thinking, do you realise most of the people here went to Never Never Land?"

"Sure. Nearly everyone at Laburnum High went there. Except for Oz; he had home tuition."

"They're all — we've all *changed*."

"Be pretty sad if we hadn't."

"It's weird," I blurted out. "Everything's changing: Oz is breaking out and James is getting strange, teachers are turning into people, so that you start feeling sorry for them. And look at Tatts Logan — he used to be a tough, and now he's a dad in a suit with two little kids —"

"He's still a tough, though."

"Yeah, but it's scary how —"

"No, it's not. It's *interesting*, everything's interesting. Did I tell you about —" she broke off, peering over the top of the stove, through the window and down the back yard. It was dark and empty, except for a little light gleaming down beyond the clothesline. "Hey!" she cried. "Someone's down in Macca's bungalow. Let's go and take a look."

"Do you think we should? It might be private."

"I like to see what's going on around the place," replied Kelly briskly. "You only live once, and like I told you, everything's interesting."

The bungalow was an old garden shed done up as a granny flat; no grannies slept there, the place belonged to Macca. We all rather envied him that private shelter, and the twenty yards of distance it put between him and his parents. It was something we all dreamed about, that desirable possession estate agents referred to as "a separate entrance". He could slip out at night and get back home at seven in the morning and his parents wouldn't even notice.

Kelly was standing on tiptoe, gazing unashamedly through the grimy little window. "Just look at this!" she cried.

"What is it?"

"Come and see. Oh, come *on*, Al, it's nothing sordid, nothing X-rated." She clapped me on the shoulder and the force of the blow sent me lurching right up against the glass; Kelly would have been a great asset to the school football team, but the coach was a conservative type and wouldn't let her join up.

The scene inside the bungalow was definitely for

general exhibition: you might even call it family comedy. It featured Macca's parents, Mr and Mrs Macleod, blankets draped around their shoulders, uncomfortably perched on two old deck-chairs, a small folding table between them. They were having a game of cards. You could practically see their teeth chattering; it was freezing in the shed. Macca wasn't allowed to have a heater in case he set himself alight and his folks got charged with child neglect.

"Isn't that sweet?" crooned Kelly. "Sort of — peaceful. My parents always fight when they play cards."

"Mine don't know how to," I replied. "Play cards, I mean."

Mrs Macleod glanced up from her game and spotted us. "Is it over?" she asked eagerly, hurrying to the door, her blanket trailing behind her. "Are they going home? Is it all right to come inside?"

"No one's going home yet, Mrs Macleod," I informed her. "It's only twelve o'clock."

"They don't start going home till one," added Kelly. "Four if they clean up."

"Oh, they don't have to clean up," cried Mrs Macleod. "Tell them they don't have to stay behind for that, will you Kelly? I'll clean up. It'll be quicker that way, I know where everything is."

Where everything *was*, I thought.

"Why don't you come inside?" Kelly asked. "It's freezing out here."

"Oh, we don't want to spoil the party," murmured Mrs Macleod. "We promised Andy we'd be out till two o'clock, only the restaurant closed at eleven and they pushed us out; we didn't have anywhere else to go."

"You should have gone to a disco," I suggested. "They stay open till seven in the morning."

"Elton doesn't like the music," whispered Mrs Macleod, glancing towards her shivering husband. "It makes his ears go funny. A sort of ringing which goes on and on, hours after the music has stopped. Like an echo. And anyway," she added, "we're not quite the right age for discos."

"They've got ones for old, I mean, older people," I said. "With old-fashioned music — softer, you know."

"I think you've got to be single for discos," Mrs Macleod said shyly. "Elton and I are married, you know."

"Poor things," remarked Kelly, as we crunched back over the frosty grass. "Fancy having to spend Saturday night in a freezing shed just because your kid is having a party."

"Yeah," I agreed. "Mrs Macleod's lips were turning blue." It was odd, I thought, how you could feel sorry for other people's parents but never for your own. If I'd been able to shift the Capsellas out of the house for a whole Saturday night I wouldn't have cared if they'd turned blue all over.

13

Lime Koola

Lou was waiting in the kitchen, grinning to himself. "Hey, guess what!"

"What?"

"You know that kiddy-plaque I lifted off Oz's door? Guess where I put it!"

"Where?"

"There was this girl flaked out in Mr Macleod's den. Emma Chipper, I think it was, but you couldn't be sure, she had a coat over her face — well, I took a shoelace out of one of Mr Macleod's desert boots, threaded the plaque on it, and hung it round her neck, so the thing was lying on her . . . chest. Get it? 'Oz sleeps here'!" He chortled.

"Big joke, that's the kind of thing Dad would have got up to when he was a kid. Anyway, look, have you seen Oz? We've got to get him back on time or the Padkins will have the cops out."

"Last time I saw him was a few hours back; he was slumped up against the drinks table. Looked a bit odd."

"Shit! You mean he was drunk?"

"Could have been. Anyway, he's disappeared, I haven't seen him for ages. He might have gone home."

"He wouldn't do that, he said he was coming with us. We'd better find him fast; it's nearly one o'clock now."

The crowd was thinning a little; some of the kids had moved on to other parties, others had drifted off to McDonald's before it closed. Some, I guessed, were dozing in the Macleods' back rooms.

"He might have gone to get a hamburger," suggested Lou.

"Not him, he likes pies, remember? I'll bet he's conked out somewhere." We wandered down the hall, peering into bedrooms that were full of huddled shapes and smoke and giggles.

"Garnet was looking for you," murmured Lou.

"Yeah. Is she still here?"

"She's gone home. Someone told her you and Kelly Krake were cuddling up together in the kitchen."

"We weren't 'cuddling up'! It was just that we were in a small space, you know that narrow bit between the fridge and the stove. It was a tight squeeze, that's all."

"Tight squeeze, heh heh."

"Look, we were just *talking* — about Never Never Land."

"Never Never Land!"

"Listen, will you —"

"Keep your shirt on, I believe you; I hope no girls get a crush on me. Lucky I'm so funny-looking, as Mr Santini always says. — Hey, there he is! *Oz!*"

Oz didn't respond. He was lying flat on his back on the floor of the Macleods' bedroom, his feet stuck in the door of the wardrobe, his head propped up against the end of the bed. Something had happened to the shagpile hairpiece; it was fixed on sideways now, from ear to ear, like those plastic headbands little girls use to keep their curls in place. Lou tried to put it right way round, but the thing wouldn't move; it was stuck fast to the top of Oz's prickly skull.

"Some joker's been busy with the superglue," he remarked. "Poor old Oz, he'll have to soak his head in a bucket of water for a couple of days."

"Shut up, will you? Help me get him up; he's really heavy."

"Must be Glix's pies."

"Wha—" As we took hold of his arms, Oz began to wake up. He looked round the room blearily, and seemed puzzled by what he saw. "Where's Mum?"

"Waiting for you. It's nearly one o'clock, you're at Macca's party, remember?"

"A party? Why am I in a bedroom?"

"You must have passed out."

"Passed *out?*"

"What was it?" I prompted.

"What was what?"

"What were you drinking?"

A dazed smile illuminated his face. "Lime Koola! I haven't had it for years; my Aunty Florence used to buy it for me when I was little and Mum let her take me out. We'd go to Coles Cafeteria and have these marvellous lunches: sausage rolls and chips and jellycake with cream, and Lime Koola."

"I don't think this is the same kind of drink at all, Oz. It's Cooler, not Koola; it has alcohol in it, and no limes."

He blinked at us. "You know, I wondered why it wasn't green. Alcohol, eh?" He shook his head. "I've been *drinking.*" Raising a feeble hand he dabbed weakly at the shagpile. "Something's wrong with my head. Hey — hey! It's on the wrong way, it's *sideways!*" His eyes bulged with real terror.

"Calm down," Lou told him. "It's just your hairpiece, it fell off and someone's stuck it back on sideways. Your head's okay, it's straight enough — on the outside, anyway."

"Come on, let's go," I urged.

It was well after one o'clock now, and at the rate Oz was slouching along, one step at a time, propped up between us, I reckoned we'd be lucky to reach his joint by three. The Padkins would be in a frenzy. They'd go round and wake up the Capsellas, and probably the Pines as well, there'd be teenagers' parents wandering the streets of Laburnum all night.

"Feeling okay, Oz?" asked Lou.

"Wonderful!"

"Not sick or anything? You don't want to be sick, do you? If you do you'd better —"

"Never felt better in my life," mumbled Oz. "Just a bit sleepy. Ve-ery sleepy. Can't we sit down for a minute? There's a nice fence there, a nice little brick fence with a flat top — let's sit there. Look, there's a stork in the garden, let's talk to the stork."

"No time, Oz," I said. "Besides, it can't talk, it's just made of plaster. And your mum's expecting you, she might be worried."

"Nah," replied Oz. "She's all right, my mum. She's changed. It was that course she did, she didn't come first in it like she'd expected, she came —" he giggled "— last." He clutched at my sleeve. "She's okay really, though she did stop me going out to Coles Cafeteria with Aunty Florence. She said it wasn't, wasn't —"

"Good wholesome food," I supplied.

"We're nearly home," puffed Lou. "There's Glix's milk-bar."

"Let's get a pie," Oz urged. "I'm hungry again."

"No pies."

"He's closed, anyway," I added. "*Really* closed this time."

"There's a light," insisted Oz.

"*No!*" Hauling him under the armpits, we hustled him along past the front of the shop. There was a rumour about that if you peered through the shop windows late at night, you could see Glix still in there, talking to the chocolate bars, or even dancing slowly round the floor with the cardboard figure of the Alpine Dairymaid. I felt I wasn't ready for a scene like that.

"I'd *like* a pie," whined Oz, peering back over his shoulder. "I'd very much like a pie." He went on whining all the way down Pepperel Street, like a little kid being dragged away from a toyshop. We hurried him past Tatts Logan's place, where there was a light showing and you could hear the weary bawling of Tatts's voice singing the twins to sleep with football songs. It wouldn't do for Tatts to see us straggling home from a party at three in the morning while he was boxed up singing lullabies. He might think we'd come that way on purpose, just to needle him.

When we reached the Padkins' gate, Oz refused to go inside. He seemed anxious to draw the evening out, and I didn't blame him; there was a light in the living-room and Mrs Padkin's long shadow was pacing up and down behind the curtains.

"That's Mum," said Oz unnecessarily.

"What'll you do?" asked Lou.

"Well —" he pondered. "Look, I think the best thing is, I'll just lie down here on the nature strip and take a little nap. Soon as I wake up I'll slip inside, she'll be in bed by then."

"Right." It didn't seem such a bad idea to me, the grass was comfortable enough, and he couldn't really come to any harm lying on a nature strip in a quiet back street in Laburnum. It was ten to three; if Mrs Padkin hadn't called the cops by now, she obviously wasn't going to. A bit more pacing and she'd sensibly conclude that Oz had just slept over at Macca's place. Besides, Lou and I had our own Watchdogs to worry about. So we left him there, stretched out peacefully on the grass, and headed home by the shortcut through the reserve.

The moon was bright, but it was dead quiet and rather spooky in there, with the big gums casting long black shadows over the jogging track. Although the houses in Pepperel Street were only a few yards away there was a definite feeling of being miles from anywhere, and we fell silent, quickening our steps.

"Hey!" Lou grabbed at me.

"What is it?"

"Look!" He pointed downwards: in the centre of the track there was a small red point of light, a burning cigarette.

We looked around nervously; anyone might have been behind those trees, watching us; someone *was* about: discarded cigarettes don't burn all that long. Lou bent down and began scrabbling about in the woodchip.

"What are you looking for?"

"Sticks, Y-shaped sticks," he gabbled. "It could be that prowler who came to your window, the one with the big feet whose name starts with Y."

"But that was only James."

"Oh *God* — here's one, look!" He thrust it under my nose.

"Well, sure, but you get lots of Y-shaped sticks. I mean, that's the shape twigs come in. That's why James has such a big collection of cigarette holders."

"It's *him*, I tell you. Not James, the prowler!"

A breeze blew, the shadows danced over the path, we turned and ran and we didn't stop running until we'd reached my gate.

"Who do you think would be out at this time of night?" Lou asked, his face ashy-pale in the moonlight.

"Could be James, out for a breath of fresh air."

"But James would have spoken to us."

"Might have wanted to give us a scare. He was probably shitty about missing Macca's party."

"But he didn't want to come! Anyway, I don't think it's him, he's not that off."

Off — the word sounded unpleasantly in my ears. I recalled Mrs Capsella's perpetual warning: "There are funny people about."

"Could have been a jogger," I suggested unconvincingly.

"Joggers don't smoke," said Lou. His house was only a few yards on up the road, but he seemed unwilling to walk that distance alone. I didn't really blame him. "Want to sleep over at my place?" I asked.

"Nah, I didn't tell Mum. She might go out to look for me and then that big-footed man might be lurking somewhere, waiting . . . look, you just stand here by your gate and wait till I get inside mine, right?"

"Right."

It didn't take long, he covered the fifty yards in record time, and I turned gratefully into my own drive.

Mrs Capsella was taking a turn on the terrace. Watchdog!

"Looking for someone?" I inquired.

She seemed embarrassed. "Just the cat."

"We don't have a cat."

"Next door's cat, I mean. I thought I heard it howling."

"Got mugged, did it? Had a car accident? Someone pump it full of heroin while it was dancing in a disco?"

She pretended she hadn't heard.

14

Bad Dreams

"Oswald! Oswald!"

Oswald Padkin was running a long-distance hurdle race: thin and white and knobbly in his grey school racing shorts and the vest with *Laburnum High School* blazoned on the back, he was clearing the obstacles easily, gracefully, furlongs ahead of the nearest struggling competitor. The mothers were cheering him on: mothers and fathers and grannies and teachers, and the mighty roar of King Arthur boomed out above the crowd. "A credit to the School!" he was shouting.

One hundred metres from the finish line a weird thing happened. Oswald began to change: he grew taller and heavier, his small, pointed face broadened and strengthened, a bristly stubble formed upon his chin, the Brillo-pad hair thinned and fell away and a real orange mohawk rose proudly from the ridge of his skull. The school sports gear transformed itself into a spangled tank top and full pink satin harem pants, the racing shoes became imported Doc Martin boots . . .

But the boots weighed him down, he lost speed, the harem pants tangled in the hurdle bars, he crashed to the ground and lay still, and the sports field changed magically into the neatly mown grass of the Padkins' nature strip. The cheering voices dwindled to cries of alarm and disgust; one voice rose shrilly above the rest — not King Arthur's, but the voice of my own mother, Mrs Capsella. *"Oswald!"* she mewed. *"Oswald!"*

I struggled awake. All night long, before that dream began, I'd been haunted by two images: the red cigarette end glowing on the track in the reserve, and the limp, defenceless form of Oswald, stretched out on the nature strip, deeply asleep. In the shock of waking and hearing his name, those two images suddenly came together: Oswald and the prowler. After Lou and I had gone, the strange big-footed man could have crept back through the reserve, turned up Pepperel Street and come upon Oswald, laid out flat, a ready victim. I jerked up from the pillows in a panic.

"What's happened to him?" I gasped.

Mrs Capsella was standing in the doorway. "Are you awake, Al? Mrs Padkin rang up and —"

"Has something happened to him?" I repeated hoarsely.

She frowned, silent, and I knew Oz was all right. If he'd been mugged she'd certainly have come out with the news at once.

"No," she answered primly. "But it *could* have. Why on earth did you boys leave him lying on the nature strip?"

"Gee, Mum, he was tired, he wanted to flake out on the grass and we couldn't talk him out of it."

"Did you let him drink?"

"Let him? He's not a baby, Mum. He had a bit too much Cooler and it made him sleepy; he thought it was some kind of lime cordial his Aunty Flo used to buy him in Coles Cafeteria."

There was a little gasp of concern from the hallway, and I guessed Mr Capsella was standing there, eavesdropping on the conversation. In his line of business at the University my father came across quite a few heavy drinkers and the experience had unsettled him. Normally he was rather hazy about the details of modern life, but a year or so back he'd fallen asleep in front of the television and woken up in the middle of a documentary on teenage alcoholism. At first he'd thought it was a late night horror movie, but gradually it had dawned on him that the thing was real. He'd never been quite the same since; the film had preyed on his mind: he was always checking the levels of the bottles in the drinks cabinet, and I'd once caught him poking around in the back of my wardrobe: he claimed he was looking for a biro.

But Mr Capsella was barking up the wrong tree. I'd have a can or two at a party — no one wants to look like a freak — but I wasn't really into drink; the marks on the bottom of some of my school assignments suggested I shouldn't be exposed to further brain shrinkage.

"I hope *you* didn't drink any Cooler," muttered Mr Capsella anxiously, coming forward to join my mother in the doorway.

"I wouldn't touch the stuff," I said truthfully. "It's foul."

"What were you drinking?"

"Um, cider."

"Was it alcoholic?"

"Gee Dad, how should I know? I couldn't see the label, there was too much smoke in the air. Don't you know that nagging is bad for potential addicts? You're enough to turn a person into an alcoholic." I turned to Mrs Capsella. "What did Oz's mum say?" I asked. "Was she mad?"

"She was just upset. When Oswald didn't get home in time she waited and waited —" here Mrs Capsella sighed, recalling, I suppose, her own totally unnecessary

87

vigils "— and then she went out to look for him in her car. And you know what?"

"I'm waiting to hear."

"She nearly ran over him! If he'd been just that little bit closer she'd have driven right over his feet! Honestly, Al, you should have made sure he got safely inside the house."

"He wouldn't go. I think he was a bit worried about the reception committee inside."

"You could have put him inside the fence, at least, on his own lawn. Anything could have happened: the police might have come by and arrested him for vagrancy. Next time you go out with him, just be a bit more thoughtful; Oswald's an innocent boy."

She was right on that score. "He'd never even had a pie," I remarked.

"What?"

"Oh, nothing. Did Mrs Padkin say anything about not letting him go out with us again?" Looking after Oz could get to be a problem.

"She was too upset, poor thing. I couldn't really understand what she was saying." A puzzled expression crossed her face. "She kept on talking about science fiction."

"Sci-fi, eh?"

"Does that mean anything to you?"

"Not a thing."

There was a sudden stealthy chuckle from Mr Capsella. "Legless," he chortled.

We stared at him, as we often did.

"Legless," he repeated, gasping for breath. "Get it? If Mrs Padkin had run over Oswald's feet he'd be legless!"

We were silent.

"Don't you get it? Legless — *drunk?*" He doubled up like a kid in Year Seven.

"Good one, Dad," I said.

Mr Capsella took this literally and a delighted smile shone from his face. Greatly encouraged, he embarked upon another joke. "Have you heard about the Irish bank robber —" he began, but I cut him short. "Love to, Dad, but I've got to do some homework this morning and all these jokes, you know, they kind of distract me, create the wrong atmosphere for serious —"

"Oh," he breathed, heavily contrite. "Sorry, I'll leave you to it."

"No worries, Dad. If you're still marking those essays in the TV room, keep the set turned down, will you?"

He shuffled off. Mrs Capsella waited till he was out of earshot, and then she whispered, "There was another call for you."

"When?"

"Last night, about one o'clock." She lowered her voice even further. "It was a girl."

The reason she was whispering was that Mr Capsella was almost as anxious about girls as he was about drink. I suspected he'd fallen asleep in front of the television again, woken up in the middle of an X-rated movie about teenage nymphos, and thought it was a documentary.

"Garnet?" I asked.

"Yes."

"What did she want?"

"Just to know if you were home or not. She seemed to think you might have gone off with someone called Kelly. Seen her home, you know," she added awkwardly.

"Listen Mum, Oswald was the only person I saw home."

89

"Oh, I know that. I told her you were probably just taking *him* home, but she didn't seem convinced."

"You didn't give her Oz's phone number, so she could find me, did you?"

"Of course not, she'd have woken up the Padkins. I just —" she hesitated guiltily.

"You just what?"

"I just had a little talk with her."

There was a sudden burning sensation in my stomach; if I'd had a stomach ulcer it would have burst right at that moment. Mrs Capsella had had a little talk with *Garnet!* I thought of all those soppy stories my mother wrote, they all had the same plot: whatever the obstacles, the girl always got her man.

"Is something wrong?"

I didn't answer all at once, it's best to be quiet when you've had a shock like that.

"What's the matter? Have you got a headache?"

"You didn't tell Garnet that I was keen on her or anything, did you?" I asked faintly.

"As if I'd do a thing like that! I just told her you'd be happy to go to her party."

I frowned. I hadn't heard that Garnet was having a party. Her parents, like my own, never went away for weekends.

"There's nothing wrong with that, is there?" Mrs Capsella asked. "You're always going to parties, so I couldn't think of any reason why you wouldn't want to go to this one. It's at three o'clock next Sunday."

"*Three?*"

"That's what she said."

"Listen, Mum, you must have got it wrong. No one has a party at three in the afternoon. Only little kids."

"It's a tea-party; she's going to make a cake."

90

I felt the burning sensation returning; perhaps it really was an ulcer. "Is anyone else going?"

She shrugged. "I didn't ask; she might have thought I was prying."

"Geez Mum, why did you have to say I'd go? There won't be anyone else there, just me. Just me and Garnet."

"It's only an afternoon-tea thing; I don't see what you're so worried about."

"Look, if any of the kids find out about it, they'll think I'm Garnet's boyfriend or something."

"Why on earth should they think that? Just because a girl asks you to tea, and you go, it doesn't mean you're her boyfriend."

It was obvious from this remark that Mrs Capsella hadn't gone to a school like mine.

"You don't understand," I wailed. God, she was an idiot. This was the most terrible thing she'd done to me, it was worse than the time in Grade Four when she'd tried to fix me up with ballet classes.

"Honestly, Al, you're being ridiculous. Anyone would think the poor girl drank blood or something; she's not Dracula's daughter, she won't eat you alive. Anyway, you won't be all on your own, her parents will be there."

"Will they?" It was the first time in years I'd been glad to hear someone's parents would be on deck. "Are you sure they're going to be there? Did she tell you?"

"I asked: I thought if it was going to be a family affair you might take something for Mrs Disher, a bunch of flowers, perhaps."

I couldn't help smiling to myself. A bunch of flowers! As if any kid would do that! And in broad daylight, too — if Mrs Capsella stopped bullshitting to herself and just thought rationally for five seconds she'd realise that in all the time we'd lived in Laburnum she'd never once seen a teenager, even a girl, carrying a bunch of flowers along the street. Just as she'd never seen a little kid in a pinafore with her satchel on her back, walking along the road with a big rosy apple for the teacher in her hand.

"Mum, kids don't do that kind of thing any more, take flowers and stuff; they probably never did, except in books." The only person I could even dimly imagine walking out in public with a bunch of flowers in his hand was Dasher's ex, Casper Cooley, and he wouldn't be able to find anyone to give them to.

When she noticed me smiling to myself, Mrs Capsella grew more confident. She lost her guilty manner and said briskly, "Well, there you are, you see. It's a perfectly harmless little occasion. But if you feel it might be dangerous, why then, just ring up Garnet —"

"What will I say?"

"Say?" Her briskness vanished suddenly. "Don't you like her?" she asked uneasily.

"Yeah, sure, Garnet's all right, I guess."

She was, too. As a matter of fact, Garnet was one of the best-looking girls in the school, the kind of girl hoons waved and whistled at from the open windows of beat-up Kingswoods, the kind of girl even Tatts Logan would admire. He'd go off his nut with jealousy if he saw me walking down the street with Garnet Disher. And she wasn't just good-looking, she was nice as well. I'd known her since Never Never Land, she was kind and clever and just about everyone liked her. I mean, *I* liked her, that is, until she started liking me in that particular way.

"What did *you* say to boys when they asked you out and you didn't want to go?" I asked Mrs Capsella.

"I don't remember," she lied.

"Yes, you do."

"No, I *don't*. Well, I suppose I just said I was busy that night, washing my hair or something."

"But you couldn't be washing your hair all the time. Say if some guy asked you out on Thursday night, and you said you had to wash your hair, then he'd say, 'What about Saturday?' What would you do then?"

"I'd say I'd think about it, and then I'd just — keep out of his way."

I could imagine that: Mrs Capsella, twenty-five years back, slipping behind a tree or the back of a building when she saw some guy hoving into view across the playground, hiding in the girls' washroom at recess, even skipping classes. I didn't want to live like that; it was the life of a fugitive, always on the run. Yet I didn't want to be mean to Garnet, I didn't like having to say *no*, straight out. It looked like you thought the girl was a dag . . .

"You can't just keep hiding —" I began, but Mrs Capsella, finding the conversation suddenly embarrassing, had vanished, sneaked off down the hall and hidden herself in her study.

All at once my throat itched, the way it does at the beginning of a cold. A cold lasted a week. If only, just this once, I could catch a cold when I wanted to, or a small dose of flu, nothing serious, just enough to keep me out of circulation until Garnet's tea-party had passed!

The phone shrilled: honest, for a moment I was scared to touch it, I felt sure it was Garnet. But it was only James.

"I'm going to be a Mormon," he informed me.

"What?" I couldn't believe my ears. If there was one thing that bothered James more than HSC exams and diseases of the brain, it was Mormons. He'd been scared

of them ever since he was a baby. "You're joking," I said weakly.

"Nope. Think about it. It's not a bad life, nothing to it, just walking round the streets knocking on doors and chatting people up."

"If they don't see you coming first."

He ignored this. "And you get a free black suit, and a bicycle, and —"

"But you always said they gave you the creeps."

"I've changed my mind." He hung up before I could protest further.

I rang Lou. "Did James tell you he's thinking of becoming a Mormon?"

"Yep."

"Don't you think it's — off?"

"Sure, but he won't go through with it. He thinks you've just got to fill in a form and you're on your bike and ready to go. When he finds out he'll have to go to Bible College for years and years he'll give it up. It's just a kind of daydream really, like when we used to think we'd run a milk-bar. — By the way, I asked him if he was in the reserve last night, and he wasn't, so that means there *is* a prowler loose."

"Could be." I felt I had more pressing problems on my mind. I passed on the news about Garnet's tea-party.

"What you should do," he suggested, "is find some really handsome guy and introduce him to Garnet."

"I don't know any really handsome guys." This was true enough, but even over the phone I could sense that Lou had taken the remark personally and was a little hurt. He was very sensitive about his appearance. "How about you?" I suggested quickly.

"I'm too young for that sort of thing."

"You're only two months younger than me."

He ignored this. "The other thing you could do," he said, "is get to know her better, or rather, let *her* get to know you better. You know what they say, 'Familiarity breeds contempt'."

"Rack off!" He didn't take it seriously because it wasn't happening to him. I just wished some girl would take a fancy to Lou: someone like Chukka Malloy, the netball captain; she'd make him go and watch her practise on Saturday afternoons; he might even have to join the cheer squad.

15

Under Stress

I read once that colds have a psychological cause: you catch them when you're weak and under stress. There must have been some truth in that, because by Sunday evening the itch in my throat had turned into a ragged rawness; I couldn't speak, and when I tried to swallow it felt as though I had a golf ball lodged halfway down my neck. Mrs Capsella made me a hot lemon drink and stood beside the bed while I drank it. I knew she was waiting to take the cup away and wash it in boiling water so the germs wouldn't spread, she was callous like that. I caught myself imagining, just for a moment, how Garnet would have brought me lemon juice and aspirin and not worried in the least about contagion. I snuffed the image out, for I knew that if Garnet had actually been there, smoothing the sheets and wiping my forehead with a cool cloth, I'd have felt desperate to get away.

I had bad dreams that night and for the rest of the week, when Mrs Capsella insisted that I stay in bed. Dreams about girls, but not the sort guys like Broadside Williams might have enjoyed. These girls were fully dressed; they were the ones in my year at school, Garnet and Emma Chipper and Melissa Pole and Cherry Clagg. They were in a huddle by the school canteen, heads down like the members of a rugby scrum, giggling and whispering. Occasionally they'd pause, fall silent, and glance across the playground in my direction, and then a wave of fresh giggling would burst out. I knew they were talking about me; they knew something about me that I didn't know . . . what was it?

The strange thing about the dream was its ordinariness: it didn't seem like a dream at all, but a chunk of real life. I could see the graffiti on the walls of the shower block, the new lawn that Mr Meeker, the school caretaker, had foolishly planted in the lower courtyard, the delicate green shoots already trodden down and clumps of sticky mud showing through. You could see Meeker's face, sad and abused, looking out from the window of his little cubby hole beside the boiler room. Mossy Crocket was standing all by herself in a little cloud of cigarette smoke on the verandah, Mr Tweedie was taking playground duty, his head lowered over the pages of a mathematical journal, while two metres away from him, two Year Ten toughs were trying to strangle a Year Seven. The sense of ordinariness scared me: I felt it wasn't a dream but a vision of the future, the very near future, next Monday lunch-time, after Garnet's tea-party.

I tossed around beneath the sheets. Why did Garnet worry me so much? What was I scared of? Was it sex? Was I scared that Garnet would squeeze up to me on her parents' sofa, expecting the kind of action I didn't even want to think about? I knew plenty in theory, of course; you couldn't get through four years of high school in the company of the kind of kids we had and not know all the finer points. But theory was different from the real thing. And it wasn't just inexperience: the simple fact was that I just didn't fancy Garnet Disher. I just didn't feel drawn. When I saw her my heart lurched and my stomach sank, but that wasn't love, it was fear. If she stopped ringing me up and passing notes in school, if she fell for some other guy, I wouldn't be jealous — I'd be relieved.

"Well," remarked Mrs Capsella on Friday, grinning to herself as she caught sight of the "Get Well" card Garnet had sent in the mail, "lucky that cold came along, wasn't it? Heaven-sent, really; now you can weasel out of the tea-party."

"I'm not weaselling out of anything," I replied stiffly. "I'm going."

I was, too. You had to be firm, I decided. You had to talk things over in a mature fashion, get the facts straight. After all, the sooner Garnet gave up on me, the sooner she could get cracking on some more receptive guy. And I wouldn't be slinking about feeling guilty, worried the girls were giggling about me because they thought I was a slow mover, or the kind of jock who'd rather spend his Saturday nights watching footy replays with a box of stubbies than go out with a girl.

I psyched myself up and dialled Garnet's number. "I'm better," I announced. "I can make it on Sunday."

"Great! What's your favourite cake? I'll get Mum to whip it up."

"Don't go to any trouble," I said hurriedly. "Biscuits will do fine."

"No, I'll get her to make a devil's food cake, with *real* chocolate." She paused. "Can I ask you something personal, Al?"

"Go ahead," I told her, my voice dribbling out in an Oz-like squeak.

"Did Kelly Krake send you a 'Get Well' card?"

"Uh, no."

"I saw her in the newsagents, looking through them. She made me so *mad!* Are you sure she didn't send one?"

"Positive. Mum would have opened it and shown me."

"Perhaps she forgot."

"Mum wouldn't forget a thing like that."

"Oh, well —" she gave a big sigh of relief. "See you on Sunday."

"Seeya," I echoed gloomily.

16

Keeping Fit

The reserve was a peaceful place on Sunday afternoons, full of kids playing and families out on suburban bushwalks. Sometimes you'd even see Tatts Logan there, taking the twins for a stroll, holding their little hands in his big gorilla paws, telling them stories of his glorious youth. It was a touching sight, but one you'd be unwise to linger on too long: Tatts hated being caught out in his gentler moments.

Garnet lived in one of the hilly streets across the creek. At night you could see the lights of those houses, high up, twinkling through the trees. From the top of the hill you had a perfect view into the backyards of all the houses along my street: I glanced back and there was James, stretched out on a rug on his lawn, an open book beside him, the wind riffling the pages. He appeared to be asleep. Mrs Pine, her face shaded by a blue sunhat, was digging in her fern garden, and old Mr Bispin was taking a turn with his Flymo.

Quite a few of the girls from our school lived in these high houses, and I realised sharply that if I'd been down there in my own yard, they'd have been able to see my every move. They could have been watching me for years; no wonder I felt those groups of girls outside the canteen knew things about me. As I stood there, appalled, I saw Lou come out onto his back porch and call Mrs Pine to the telephone. He didn't yell, he used his normal speaking voice, yet I could hear every single word: "Mum, someone's set Uncle Herbie's garbage can alight again and he wants you to go over and hold his hand!" Living in our street was like living in a department store window at Christmas time. From now on I'd have to spend more time indoors.

As I turned into Arcadia Avenue, which led on into Garnet's street, I saw two Year Nine girls grinning at me from a front verandah. The moment I was out of sight I guessed they'd rush inside to the telephone: they'd know where I was headed. Word gets round.

I began to rehearse the speech I'd prepared for Garnet. I wouldn't deliver it the moment I walked through the door, that would be too abrupt — I'd wait a bit, till things started getting sticky. "You're a great girl, Garnet — I like you a lot, but not in *that* way." It sounded queerly familiar, as if I'd heard the words before, though certainly I hadn't: no friend of mine would say something like that. Perhaps I'd heard them in a film, or read them in a book — a book about a prick. For that's what struck me now: they were the words of a prick, some slithery private-school type with a mod haircut and bopper's clothes.

"I like you, but not in *that* way." Geez, I couldn't say that, it was nasty, like hanging up the phone on a lonely bore. It saved your skin, but there was something distinctly inhuman about it.

As I paced out the last few slow steps of Arcadia Avenue, a guy came loping round the corner, a tall, gangly man, slightly stooped, with reddish hair that was getting a bit thin on top, and big feet. He was smoking a cigarette, taking low, slow puffs and blowing the smoke out from his nostrils, like a big horse breathing in the

101

cold. His eyes had a guilty, slightly apprehensive expression which deepened when he spotted me. He hid the cigarette behind his back like a nervous ten-year-old: sensitive about his filthy habit, I figured.

"Hi," he murmured, sounding as if he knew me.

"G'day," I replied, slightly puzzled. He wasn't familiar to me at all. We stood staring at each other and the cigarette smoke plumed out gently from behind him, as if the back of his shirt was on fire. I wished he'd move along, he was blocking my path, and his queer nervousness was making me edgy.

"Nice day," I said, breaking the awkward silence.

"Oh, great." He grinned sheepishly and lowered his voice. "Listen, I'd be grateful if you didn't mention seeing me."

"Oh, right."

Nodding pleasantly, the guy ambled on down the street, shifting his cigarette to the front again, out of my sight. What was that about? I wondered. Who on earth did he think I was going to mention him to? There were weirdos loose all over the streets: he was probably some poor kid's parent. At least the Capsellas kept inside the house, didn't wander round the neighbourhood drawing attention to themselves and begging strangers not to notice them.

In the front yard of Garnet's house there was a lady laid out flat like a corpse on the lawn. The sight didn't alarm me; there was a fitness craze going on around Laburnum, and I could see that Mrs Disher was alive all right; her stomach, beneath the blue tracksuit, was gently heaving up and down. As I came closer I saw that she was attached to one of those plastic gut-buster jobs, the kind they sell on TV for $19.99 with a free gold bracelet thrown in.

"Hi," I said, and she opened her eyes, startled, and

tried to get up. It wasn't all that easy with her arms and legs attached to the gut-buster. The elastic cords strained dangerously as she struggled into a sitting position. "You must be Al," she puffed, red-faced.

I nodded.

"I'm Glenys Disher, Sophie's mother." She grinned and added brightly, "you're keen."

"Keen?"

"Early — it's only ten past three. Sophie wasn't expecting you till four."

Four! Trust Mrs Capsella to get the time wrong. I'd planned my arrival for ten minutes past the hour, just so I wouldn't seem eager nor all that unwilling. Now I simply looked like a fool.

"She's still taking her bath, I think," Mrs Disher went on, and at once this weird idea flashed into my head that Garnet would suddenly appear on the veran-dah, quite naked, or wrapped in a flimsy towel, her hair wet and faint steam rising from her skin. I was appalled by the vision: there was definitely something wrong with me; half the kids in Year Eleven would give away their Finals tickets to see Garnet, or any other girl, in the raw. And I hadn't always been like this; back in Grade Three, when Si Leyland bored a hole in the wall between his bedroom and the family bathroom and charged us all twenty cents to view his mother taking a bath, I'd paid up just like everyone else; I'd even enjoyed the spec-tacle. It was different now.

Mrs Disher wrenched her feet from the gut-buster and stood up, brushing shreds of grass from her tracksuit. "I feel a bit nervous of this thing," she remarked, look-ing down at the exercise machine.

"They're dangerous," I said. "If the elastic snaps, you've had it, Mrs Disher. Kelly Krake's mum knocked out her two front teeth that way." I didn't add that Mrs

Krake had been forced to hide in the house until her dental plate was fixed, just in case the neighbours thought she was a victim of domestic violence.

"I've got to lose weight," sighed Mrs Disher. "Summer's coming soon, and I won't be fit to be seen on the beach unless I lose at least five kilos."

"I wouldn't worry about it, Mrs Disher, there are some really gross-looking types on the beach these days, you'd be surprised."

"I'm sure I would," she said stiffly.

"I didn't mean, uh — you could always take up jogging. Lots of mothers do that."

"Does yours?"

"No, she's too —" the word escaped me. "But Mrs Cadigorn does. Do you know Mrs Cadigorn, James's mother?"

"I've seen her around, jogging. Mostly on Friday and Saturday nights, when I take Yves out for his walk. — That's the dog, not my husband," she added. "They have the same name; it confuses people sometimes, but when Yves was a puppy, his eyes were exactly the same shade of blue as my husband's. They changed later, the puppy's eyes, that is. They went brown, Yves's stayed blue. But anyway, what were we talking about?"

"Mrs Cadigorn's jogging."

"Oh yes. You know, she always looks so *worried* when she jogs. She keeps stopping, too, and peering into peoples' houses, especially when there's a party going on. Is she all right, do you think?"

"Fine," I assured her. I wasn't going to dob James in, tell the world his mother went round disguised as a jogger, checking up on him; I knew what it was like to have Watchdog parents. "It's just that jogging can be a bit stressful if you're not used to it, and Mrs Cadigorn's just a beginner. It's better to start with brisk walking, if you're over for — I mean, thirty.''

Mrs Disher sighed. "Perhaps I should try it. I wouldn't want to lose my teeth." She glanced towards the house. "Coming inside?"

I hesitated. "Garnet mightn't be ready yet; my mother told me the wrong time."

Mrs Disher frowned when she heard the name "Garnet". "Yves and I went to a lot of trouble finding that girl a really distinguished name — Sophie's lovely, don't you think?"

"Yes," I said. "Um, I mean the *name*, that's lovely. Sophie's a lovely name, you're right there, Mrs Disher."

"Of course I am. And then she goes and changes it. Garnet! A cheap, dismal jewel; you'd think if she was that way inclined she'd have chosen Ruby, or even Emerald, wouldn't you?"

I shrugged. Privately I thought that when Garnet had properly gotten over Broadside Williams, she'd change right back to Sophie. But I didn't say this, because I had the feeling that Mrs Disher wouldn't welcome even the mention of Broadside's name. He wasn't the kind of kid who impressed parents.

"I'm early," I repeated. "I don't want to seem too —"

"Eager," Mrs Disher grinned. "Okay, tell you what, we can go for a stroll round the block, a brisk walk, like you suggested. Burn the old calories off. Besides, I want to check —" she tailed off vaguely. We'd reached the gate and I noticed her eyes darting sharply up and down the footpath, as if she was looking for someone. The street was empty, and we turned back the way I had come, walking briskly.

"I don't suppose you saw my husband on your way here?" asked Mrs Disher suddenly.

"I don't think I know what he looks like, Mrs Disher."

"Tall man, kind of stooped, bad posture. He got that way as a kid at high school, stooping over, pretending to be smaller so he wouldn't stand out; he's never lost the habit. Reddish hair, thinning a bit, blue eyes, green striped shirt, grey jeans, rather large feet." She reeled it off pat, as if she was down at the mortuary, looking for a body.

So the weirdo with the smoking habit was Mr Disher! I thought of the big feet, the queer, loping gate, the furtive way he'd asked me not to mention I'd seen him. I'd bet anything he was the prowler! Except that the name didn't start with Y; for some weird reason the guy had a girl's name, Eve.

"I think I saw him on Arcadia Avenue," I mumbled. "Heading towards the reserve."

"What was he doing?"

Poor woman, I felt sorry for her, her husband must be some kind of sex maniac, and Garnet — Garnet was the *daughter* of a sex maniac. I shivered; could that kind of madness be hereditary?

"He was — just walking."

"Was he smoking?"

"Um, I didn't notice." Funny how you get into a habit. I'd become so used to covering up for James's smoking that here I was doing it for a full-grown man. A madman at that.

Mrs Disher looked at me suspiciously. "You men all stick together."

"No, honest, Mrs Disher, I didn't notice."

"He's given up, you know. At least, he *did* give up. But I think he's taken it up again, secretly. At night you can smell smoke all through the house."

"Could be left over. Could have seeped into the

carpets and curtains, you wouldn't smell it in the day, but in the night, when the house is locked up, you'd notice. It's like that at home when my mum cooks cauliflower.''

"I suppose you could be right," said Mrs Disher, a shade guiltily. "It's just that I'm so worried about him, he's in the High Risk category, you know."

She was certainly right there, I thought, prowling was High Risk, no worries.

"Over forty-five," she went on, "slightly overweight, high-pressure job, sedentary. He won't go *near* the exercise machine, that's why I use it out on the lawn, he won't have it in the house."

"He was taking a walk just now."

Her eyes narrowed. "I've a feeling he just creeps out to sneak a smoke in the reserve."

"Oh no, he wouldn't do that." I looked down the street, terrified that Mr Disher's lank form would suddenly appear round the corner, wreathed in a cloud of smoke, making me a liar.

But he seemed to have vanished into thin air. When we passed an old man raking leaves into a bonfire, Mrs Disher inquired if he'd seen Eve that afternoon, and the old man replied that he'd noticed him running past with a bone in his mouth. I reckoned he meant Eve the dog and not Mr Disher.

When we arrived back at the house, just on four, there was old big-foot standing in the middle of the lawn, sneering down at the gut-buster.

"Ah, there you are, Yves," Mrs Disher remarked, sniffing at the air beside him. "I smell smoke."

Mr Disher blushed. "Someone's burning off," he muttered. "Old Mr Beamis. He's raking leaves, got a bit of a bonfire going."

Mrs Disher let it pass; I guess she didn't want to start

a fight in public. "This is Al," she said pleasantly. "Sophie's new friend."

"Well!" Mr Disher beamed. "This is quite an improvement, eh, Glenys? A step in the right direction." He turned to me. "You know, there was something about Sophie's former fellow I couldn't quite take to. Something I couldn't exactly put my finger on, but —"

"He was revolting," said Mrs Disher bluntly.

"Oh come now," her husband protested falsely. "Hardly as bad as that. But all the same, I can tell you, Al, I wasn't keen on my little Sophie going out with him, I didn't even like leaving her in the house while he was in it. You can never tell what a fellow like that might be capable of."

"Yes," I agreed, looking him straight in the eye. "No self-control."

He didn't flinch. "Exactly," he sighed. "A father has his little worries."

"You don't have to worry about me, Mr Disher," I assured him. "I'm not a bit interested in Sophie — I mean, not in that way."

Mr Disher beamed, but I saw his wife narrow her eyes in my direction.

"Mu-um! Da-ad!" Garnet appeared on the front steps. She was fully clothed, I noticed with relief, and her newly washed hair shone in the sunlight. She'd had it streaked, and it looked marvellous, but I didn't like to say so in case she thought I meant something by it.

"Hi, Al," she said in a softer tone, flicking a smile in my direction before she turned grimly on her parents. "You two said you were going out!"

"Out?" queried Mr Disher. "I wasn't planning —"

Garnet turned to Mrs Disher. "Mum," she wailed. "You *promised*."

"But where will we go?" her father whined plaintively. "It's too late for the movies."

"Go to a plant nursery or something."

"A plant nursery? I don't like those places; they give me —"

"No one else's parents stay home when they have friends over, do they, Al?"

I shuffled my feet on the grass. "Well, no," I lied.

"It's too old-fashioned to hang about. I'm nearly sixteen —"

Mrs Disher patted her daughter on the shoulder. "It's all right, dear, we're going. Your father was just teasing, weren't you, Yves?"

Mr Disher seemed inclined to linger, but his wife gave him a little push towards the driveway, where the family car stood glistening in a pool of Sunday soapsuds. "Look, you've nothing to worry about," I heard her whisper as Mr Disher fumbled for the keys. "This one's all right, Yves, he's a reliable person."

Garnet watched, holding her breath, as the car backed out of the driveway and moved slowly down the street. I guessed she was seized with that same terrible anxiety which always caught at me, on those rare occasions when I'd managed to lever the Capsellas out of the house for an evening: the awful fear that they'd drive round the corner, change their minds, and *come back*. I rather wished the Dishers would, but the moments passed, and the hum of the car's engine vanished into the Sunday noises of lawnmowers and garden mulchers and the voices of kids playing in the reserve. Garnet relaxed. "It's funny how parents seem to get younger as they grow older, isn't it?" she observed. "When I was six, those two would have given anything to go off and leave me with some *reliable person*."

17

"I didn't mean it that way . . ."

The sticky moment I'd anticipated on my walk up Arcadia Avenue had arrived. Garnet was sliding towards me on the sofa, and I was edging away, wishing I'd had the courage to choose a single armchair, or even one of the narrow straight-backed chairs in the corner, where there was definitely only room for one. But it had seemed uncouth at the time.

"You've got such beautiful hair, Al," she whispered, and in the silence that followed I remembered how Kelly Krake used to say this to me when we were at Never Never Land; she'd even sawn off a lock with her pink plastic cutting-out scissors and I hadn't minded a bit; I'd been tougher then.

"It's all right," I answered modestly, twisting my head out of reach. "Actually I've been thinking of dyeing it blonde."

"Too dark," said Garnet consideringly. "It'll go grey, like all those guys in Year Twelve."

It was funny how HSC took people that way: almost all the guys in Year Twelve had dyed their hair, or gone round to Caro's for a fancy cut; they wore earrings, three or four in one ear, and Booze Brothers t-shirts and washed-out tank tops; there was hardly a guy in that Year who resembled a student, they were like a gang of bookies' assistants and plumbers' mates and Bogans out on parole. They appeared to be people who'd never touched a book or heard the word 'exam': people who didn't have a worry in the world, but I knew uncomfortably that the truth was very different: they were kids who couldn't take a bath without worrying that they might be wasting time. Like James, they mightn't actually *do* the work, but they certainly fretted about it.

"What're you thinking about, Al?" asked Garnet softly.

"HSC," I replied.

It was as if a ghost had walked into the room; there was a distinct, icy chill in the air.

"Brrr," shivered Garnet. "Let's not talk about *that*, you can't relax if you think about schoolwork."

And this was the girl Ms Rock had recommended as a good influence!

"How come your dad's got a girl's name?" I asked, attempting to distract her attention.

"How do you mean?"

"Eve. Why is he called Eve?"

"It's *Yves*, it's a French name, Y-V-E-S."

"Y? Hey, have you ever noticed him slipping out at night?"

"Let's not talk about Dad."

"But —"

"*Shhh.*" She put a hand on my arm, gazing at me, misty-eyed. I was mesmerised, I couldn't think of a thing to say; it was like the bad old days in Mr Tweedie's class, only there it didn't matter, everyone gave wrong answers, and though your answer might be wrong, it was seldom dangerous. Images of the past flashed before my eyes as if I was drowning; I saw the pink bunny rug that used to cover my cot, the sandpit at Never Never Land, my grandfather Neddy Blount wrapping up his little parcels of garden rubbish, my first day at High School, walking up the corridor feeling scared and seeing good old Mossy Crocket smiling at me like someone's aunty.

I stared at Garnet's face, thinking how pretty she was, and it suddenly struck me how there were lots of good-looking people who had the idea they were ugly, people who got hung up on a single feature, who thought of themselves, in private, as Big Ears or Nosy, names they'd acquired long ago in Primary School. Garnet's ears stuck out a bit, you could see their pink rims shining through her hair; it was even possible she had a thing about them and didn't think she was pretty at all. Somehow I couldn't imagine Broadside Williams as the type to pass out compliments, he'd be more likely to say she was a dag, but he liked her anyway. He might even have called her "Big Ears", I wouldn't put it past him. He'd probably given her a complex, made her think . . .

"You're really beautiful, Garnet," I blurted, stupidly speaking my thoughts aloud.

"Oh, Al," she breathed, sliding up along the sofa again, pushing me into the arm-rest. In her eyes I could see a tiny picture of my own face, bolt-eyed and staring. I drew back. "I didn't mean it that way," I gasped.

Garnet drew back too, sharply; she bristled all over and the tips of those protruding ears turned bright scarlet. "What way?" she demanded.

"You know, like —"

"Oh, you needn't explain yourself, Al Capsella; I know what you mean all right. And if I'd known you were that kind of guy —"

"I'm not!"

She ignored me. "If I'd known you were the type who thinks, just because a girl invites him to tea, that she fancies him, I'd never have invited you in the first place!" She jumped up from the sofa and began to pace up and down the carpet with small furious steps.

"I didn't think you fancied me," I said weakly.

"I *hate* it when you can't even look at a boy in class, or talk to him *casually*, or ask him over, without everyone thinking you're mad about him — when you can't even ring someone up or write a letter, or even" — she paused for breath — "get your *hair* done, just because you want to, without some idiot thinking you've done it just for him!"

"So do I!" I cried. "I hate it when you can't talk to a girl in the playground without everyone looking at you and giggling, and when you can't walk past some girl's house in case she thinks you're passing on purpose just to get a look at her, so you have to walk miles out of your way. And — and that cake your mother made, it was great; I couldn't eat it because I was so nervous, but I didn't want to say so, in case it looked like I was keen on you!"

"Huh?"

"You know how they say people in love have no appetite."

"Oh. I wouldn't have thought that, Al."

Did she mean it? I couldn't be sure. I felt a bit safer, but I wouldn't feel entirely safe until she'd found a substitute for Broadside.

As we sat out on the front steps, eating the last of Mrs Disher's chocolate cake and watching the sun set over the reserve, I remarked casually, "You should get to know Oz Padkin, Garnet; he's really great these days."

"Oz Padkin! That nerd!"

"I know he used to be weird, but he's really breaking out now. He's great, honest! Good-looking too, now his hair's growing back."

Garnet's eyes narrowed like her mother's. I could have been an insect, laid out on a slide in the Biol lab, the way she looked at me. "Are you trying to fix me up with someone, Al Capsella?"

"Geez no, Garnet."

"Call me Sophie!"

"As if I'd try anything like that, Sophie. I just thought you might like to get to know him, as a friend; he's a really interesting person."

"You still think I fancy you, don't you? You *do* think I asked you over here because I'm keen on you, you think I'm jealous of Kelly Krake just because I asked if she bought you a 'Get Well' card!"

"No, you've got it all wrong —"

"Don't bother to lie about it."

"But I wasn't lying!" From the corner of my eye, with a wash of relief, I saw the Dishers' car gliding slowly up the drive, a forest of greenery waving from the back windows. Garnet, or rather Sophie's, face grew grim. "They're back. They were only gone" — she looked at her watch — "forty-five minutes."

"Forty-five minutes? Was that all?" It had certainly seemed longer to me, a whole little lifetime, in fact.

"Oh, shut up!"

The Dishers were unloading pots and tubs from the boot of the car. A cloud of perfume drifted across the lawn. Boronia!

"I think we'll have some of the small pots inside the house, don't you?" Mr Disher was saying. "A few on the kitchen sill, and on that small table in the hall, it will perfume the whole house." He rubbed his hands.

"You were only gone forty-five *minutes!*" bellowed Sophie.

"The place was closing, darling," said Mrs Disher mildly.

"Well, why didn't you go somewhere else? Why did you have to come back here?"

"Because we *live* here, darling."

Mr Disher looked up from the boronia and caught a glimpse of Sophie's furious face. He strolled across the lawn towards us. "Having a little tiff?" he asked cheerily. "Never let the sun go down on a quarrel."

"Shhh, dear." Mrs Disher tugged at his arm.

"Rack off, Dad," said Sophie, sounding remarkably like Broadside Williams. "Al's just going, anyway. And we weren't quarrelling; we've got nothing to quarrel about."

"Come along, Yves," urged Mrs Disher. "Help me get the rest of the plants unloaded."

Mr Disher allowed himself to be led away.

"He smells of smoke," whispered Sophie. "Did you notice? That's why he bought all that boronia, to disguise that foul habit of his."

"What habit?"

"Smoking!"

"Someone's burning off," I said. "I noticed when I was coming over. An old man down the road."

"You men stick together, don't you?"

"It's not that, I really *did* see —"

"Bye, Al," she said coolly, leaning forward and giving me a light kiss on the cheek.

"Bye," I muttered. Should I kiss her back? Did you have to return goodbye kisses? Did you look a fool if you did, or if you didn't? I floundered, standing in the pathway, paralysed, catching Mr Disher's eye as he stood by the car with a tub of boronia clutched in his arms. He looked faintly accusing. *"She* kissed *me!"* I felt like protesting, but it sounded so scummy that the protest died on my lips.

"See you at school on Monday," said Garnet casually. Perhaps she *had* lost interest in me; at least, that kind of interest. The kiss could even have been a farewell-for-ever one.

"See you at school on Monday."She'd said it so casually. Did she mean something by that? I wondered, as I set off back down Arcadia Avenue. Was she going to tell on me? Describe the afternoon's conversation to Emma and Melissa and Cherry Clagg and all the other girls who hung around the canteen? What had I said? I couldn't remember; the afternoon was a kind of blank. I'd been too paralysed for anything to sink in.

I glanced back, and saw Sophie standing by her gate. I waved, but she didn't seem to notice. There was a thoughtful, dreamy expression on her face as she looked out over the reserve towards the houses on the other side. Perhaps she was thinking of Oz.

18

"Can your parents swim?"

Saturday night was the Big Night Out for most people I knew: only the Capsellas stayed home. They slouched on the sofa in the television room, watching old black-and-white movies and arguing about whether they'd been six or seven when they'd seen them first time round. They were a depressing spectacle, and it made me feel guilty, going out and leaving them there. They were becoming housebound, and I was worried they might start turning into queer old agoraphobics like my grandparents, Pearly and Neddy Blount. Pearly wouldn't stir out of her house except to do the Thursday shopping and go to the Leagues Club on Saturday nights, and she wouldn't let Neddy go out either. Nor anyone who stayed in their house — visiting my grandparents was like doing a spell in Pentridge Gaol; Pearly got nervous if you so much as put your finger on a doorknob.

Occasionally the Capsellas did stir themselves, but they only went to this daggy hole called the Classic Theatre, where they watched exactly the same kind of movies on a wider screen. They really liked it better at home; the sofa was more comfortable than the seats at the Classic, and if the movie turned out boring they could always switch on the lights and read. Mrs Capsella could also do her knitting, which wasn't allowed at the Classic, because she made too much clack with her needles.

"Why don't you go out somewhere?" I asked them, hanging about in the doorway.

Mrs Capsella shrugged. "There's nothing on at the Classic."

"There's other places in town besides the Classic, Mum; it's a nerd's joint anyway. Why don't you go and see a proper film for a change?"

"Those *are* proper films."

"Why don't you go to a party or something?"

"I don't know anyone who has parties," sighed Mrs Capsella. "All our friends are too —" she tailed off, unable to find a word, though I could have supplied several.

"Why don't you have one here?"

"I can't be bothered cleaning up."

"You could go round to the Cooleys' place."

Mr Capsella shuddered slightly; he was rather nervous of Dasher.

"Well then, why don't you —"

"Oh, do leave us alone, Al," snapped Mrs Capsella. "We're quite happy sitting here, being nerds, as you'd put it."

"I was only trying to help!"

"We don't need help! We're not *cases*, Al, I wish I'd never let you do that Human Development course, you're beginning to sound like a social worker. Anyway, what about you? Aren't you going out tonight?"

"I'm just off to Lou's place, then we're heading out."

Her eyes took on a certain Watchdog beadiness. "Where are you going?"

I replied vaguely, as was my habit, and the habit of all

my friends. "We haven't made up our minds yet." I knew quite well where we were going, to Firestorm, a disco in town, but I couldn't tell her that, the very word "disco" upset her; she used it as a synonym for drugden. There was no point in giving her a bad night.

"We might take in a film," I mumbled.

"At the Classic?"

"Come off it, Mum, as if we'd go there!"

"They have very good films," put in Mr Capsella dozily. "Classics and documentaries."

"It's Saturday night, Dad."

"Oh, *God* —" The exclamation came from Mrs Capsella. She was staring at the television screen, where a sudden newsflash had interrupted the movie. I glanced at it, but couldn't see anything to account for the expression of deep apprehension in Mrs Capsella's eyes; it was just an item about violent rainstorms and flash flooding in the suburbs of Sydney.

I saw flat treeless streets swirling with brown floodwaters, old-fashioned shops and houses sunk to their window-sills in water, like pensioners on a picnic, paddling in the shallows of Half Moon Bay. There was something oddly familiar about those streets, but I couldn't quite place it . . . Debris floated on the torrent: twigs and bushes and sodden rafts of dead leaves and plastic waste, deck-chairs and barbecue umbrellas and even a plaster stork like the one in old Mr Norton's front garden. It bobbed convincingly in the muddy tide, its beak surfacing now and again above the water, as if it was gasping for air. I hoped Cherry Clagg wasn't watching. A bleak stone building appeared, water lapping halfway up its grim, prison-like windows.

Mrs Capsella gasped horribly; she might have been the sound effect for the drowning stork. "That's my old school!" she cried. "That's Mordant State, and that's

Essex Avenue, and Simla Street. And oh — Horatio Road!"

Horatio Road was where my grandparents lived. As we watched, fascinated, the Blounts' house appeared, a red-brick cottage with a high-walled verandah and a forbidding steel-mesh security door. The two plaster labradors sat in their usual places on the front gate-posts, smugly staring out above the flood.

Mr Capsella grinned. "Can your parents swim?" he asked cruelly.

"They said 'no casualties'," I put in hastily. "So they must be all right. And if anything had happened to them, they'd have rung up — well, somebody would have rung up."

"Not necessarily," said Mr Capsella, grinning wider. He didn't get on with the Blounts: Neddy thought he was a Red, and Pearly had never forgiven him for once attempting to call her "Mother".

"Perhaps you could ring *them* up."

"The phone wouldn't be working. And they wouldn't be in the house anyway, it must be full of water." She paused, her white face growing even paler, as she took in the significance of her own remark. "They'll need somewhere to stay," she whispered. "While the place is drying out."

The grin faded suddenly from Mr Capsella's face. "They'll be in emergency accommodation," he said quickly. "The local school, perhaps."

"It's under water, Dad."

"The Church Hall, then, the — Leagues Club."

"They can't stay in a place like that, like refugees," exclaimed Mrs Capsella. "You know how fussy Mum is, she'd never stay in a barracks!"

"Friends," Mr Capsella said wildly. "They'll be staying with friends."

"You know Pearly doesn't have friends."

"Neddy must have."

"Pearly doesn't like Neddy's friends, she doesn't really like anyone." Mrs Capsella sighed. "There's nothing else for it, they'll have to come here, we're their only relations."

"But — but Mum! Pearly's agoraphobic. She hasn't even been into town for thirty years, she'd never travel over a thousand kilometres!"

Hope gleamed for a moment in Mr Capsella's eyes, but Mrs Capsella quashed it. "She'll *have* to, it's an emergency." There was a small silence, in which I could hear Mr Capsella's breathing; it had taken on a peculiar rasping note.

"I'll have to clean out the spare room," Mrs Capsella cried. "I'll have to clean out the *whole house!* You know how neat she is, when she sees this place, she'll —"

I finished the sentence for her. "She'll freak out! No, wait, hang on a minute, Mum — with the flood and the travelling and being in a new place she'll probably be in shock; she won't notice a thing."

"Won't *notice!*" Mrs Capsella darted a withering glance in my direction. "Do you really believe that, Al?"

I thought of Pearly's sharp blue eyes, steely bright as the grim metal curlers she wore to bed at night. "Well, no."

"I might put them in your room, actually, it's bigger. And you can have the spare one."

"That spare room's full of junk, Mum. There's hardly space to swing a cat in there."

"You haven't got a cat. And you can help me clean it out if you're afraid of getting cramp."

"I could go and stay at Lou's place. He's got a spare

room and the Pines wouldn't mind. I could move in there tonight, when we get back from — the film.''

"You're staying *here!* They're your grandparents!''

Mr Capsella cleared his throat. "When exactly do you think they might be coming?''

"Oh, I don't know.'' Mrs Capsella's voice sounded tearful. "They could be on their way this very minute.'' She turned on him suspiciously. "Why do you want to know?''

"It's just that there's this conference in Tasmania —''

"I thought you weren't going to that.''

"I forgot to tell you,'' Mr Capsella muttered shiftily. "Freddy Miggs has come down with the flu, he asked me to go in his place and deliver his paper. I can hardly let the poor chap down.''

"When does this conference start?''

"Monday. But I'll have to leave tomorrow, get things organised, you know how it is.''

"You'd better go and pack, then,'' Mrs Capsella replied coldly.

"Well, yes,'' Mr Capsella brightened. "I was thinking of doing just that, before this news item came on. I was just about to tell you, in fact, when —''

"Oh, get lost!''

I hovered in the doorway. It seemed mean to desert her at this moment, but it was Saturday night, and the gang would be waiting up at Lou's place.

"It's not fair!'' wailed Mrs Capsella.

"I'll help you tidy the house tomorrow.''

"I wasn't talking about that. It's him —'' she gestured towards the next room, from which came the unmistakable sounds of hasty packing. "If *he* had parents, and they came to stay, I wouldn't run off like that, no matter how awful they were!''

Mr Capsella had the good luck to be an orphan. When he was a lad of nineteen, both his parents had perished in a mishap he romantically referred to a "boating accident". They'd sailed out onto Port Phillip Bay one Sunday morning for a spot of fishing and had never been seen again. The day had been calm, the sea still as glass, but the bodies had never been found, and neither had the boat. It sometimes crossed my mind, particularly on those occasions when Mr Capsella was entertaining my friends with a selection of *Little Folks'* jokes, that his parents might have vanished deliberately, gone to ground somewhere. Perhaps Mr Capsella hadn't been orphaned at all, but simply abandoned. It was a theory I never expounded to him; to do so would have been tactless, even cruel.

"You can't blame him," I said. "He's scared of Grandma."

"Who isn't? And for heavens' sake, when she gets here, don't call her 'Grandma'; you know how she hates it." She flung herself full-length on the sofa. "Do you realise what this is going to be like?"

I nodded dumbly.

"We'll have to have proper meals, and have them at proper times! She'll look in all the cupboards, and read my mail, and — we'll all have to be in bed by nine thirty!"

The phone shrilled.

"It's them!" I exclaimed.

And so it was.

19

A Bad Trip

The Blounts were on their way and Mr Capsella had deserted us; he was airborne, bound for Tasmania. Mrs Capsella and I had spent the whole day tidying the house, vacuuming the floors and clearing out the kitchen cupboards, dusting the skirting boards and whisking stray odds and ends out of sight.

"She's got eyes like a gimlet," grumbled Mrs Capsella. "If only these doors had *locks* — we could close off some of the rooms and say they were being painted."

Even when we'd finished and the place was neater than I'd ever seen it, I somehow knew that the house wouldn't pass muster with Pearly. I pictured my grandmother's face, sharp and beady-eyed, surmounted by a comic-strip speech balloon, "a place for everything and everything in its place" inscribed neatly inside it.

The train was due to arrive at Spencer Street at eight fifteen. It was only a thirty minute drive from Laburnum, but as Mrs Capsella fumbled for her car keys I felt this sinking sensation in my stomach: it had nothing to do with the Blounts, and a lot to do with my mother's limited driving skills. As she opened the car door a tiny silver plane passed overhead, red and green lights flashing on its wings. Mrs Capsella shook her fist at it.

"At least he could have caught the later flight," she grumbled. "Then he could have helped me pick them up at the station. He knows I hate driving through the city; it's full of one-way streets."

"Wrong-way streets," I muttered.

"What did you say?"

"Nothing." Her driver's licence wasn't really valid: it was the sort you get when you fail the test five times and they hand it over to stop you coming back again. She flung herself into the driver's seat and stared gloomily at the dashboard.

"Now you turn the key."

"I know that! I was just checking the time on the clock."

"Listen, Mum, I told you before, if you're nervous about driving, Lou has this friend Skull Murphy, he got his licence last week and he offered to drive us."

"As if I'm going to pick my parents up from the station in the company of a person called Skull!" She turned the key in the ignition; the engine rattled faintly, coughed once and died. "Look at that! The wretched thing won't even start. We'll be late, and you know what Mum's like about people being on time!"

"It won't start because it's cold; you've got to pump on the accelerator to get the petrol flowing."

"The accelerator?"

"That pedal down there on the floor, near your foot."

"Oh." She pumped vigorously for a few seconds and then turned the key. Once again there was that brief, throaty rattle, followed by heavy silence.

"Nothing's happening."

"Just a sec." I turned on the light and looked down at her feet. "That's because you're pumping on the *brake*.

The accelerator is the other pedal, the one on the right side.''

"Oh."

This time the motor sprang into life. She wrenched at the steering wheel.

"Mum! Hold on a minute!"

"What's the matter now?"

"Don't you know the difference between the brake and the accelerator?"

"Of course I do. When the car's going, I know, it's just when it's stopped that I get slightly confused."

"Are you sure about that?"

"Of course I'm sure. I've got a driving licence, haven't I?"

"Well —"

"What do you mean by that? And take your hand off the doorcatch, you're just like your father. It saps my confidence, having a passenger all ready to jump out. Just relax."

It was a bad trip, and a long one. We took a strange winding route which Mrs Capsella had worked out beforehand in the street directory, a route designed to get us to the city without having to risk a single right-hand turn. By the time we reached Spencer Street it was eight forty-five and the Daylight Express, emptied of its passengers, stood silently beside the platform. A solitary porter was sweeping out the carriages; there was no sign at all of the Blounts.

"They've gone," I said.

"Gone? Where would they go?"

I shrugged. "Back home?"

"Don't be silly." Mrs Capsella wandered up the platform, peering in through the windows of the empty train.

"Perhaps they decided not to come after all," I said.

All along, I'd been having this difficulty imagining Pearly and Neddy Blount actually arriving in a strange city. It was over a quarter of a century since they'd ventured outside Harris Park, their Sydney suburb, and it was almost impossible to picture them outside the confines of the little house in Horatio Street. To expect them here, on the platform of Spencer Street, Melbourne, five hundred miles from home (they still thought in miles), seemed almost bizarre.

Mrs Capsella approached the porter. "Have you seen an old couple?" she asked.

He paused in his sweeping, leaned on his broom, and grinned at us. "Old couple of what?" he inquired.

"A pair of elderly people, mate," I said coldly.

"Small, were they?"

"Well, yes, I suppose you could say that," Mrs Capsella replied.

The porter grinned again.

"So where are they, mate?" I asked.

He twirled his broom, scooping up a stray chip packet. "They waited here a bit," he said, "and they waited some more, and when no one showed up they went off upstairs. The old lady needed a cup of tea. She was going on a bit about people never knowing the time of day, or the day of the week, or what year —"

Mrs Capsella foolishly thanked him and we hurried upstairs. The Blounts were there, ensconced at a table in front of the television, watching a program on iceskating. Or at least Neddy was watching, Pearly was slumped on her chair, her tiny hands clasped round a polystyrene mug of steaming tea, as if for comfort. Her eyes were closed and her pink woolly cardigan, slightly rumpled, gave her a fluffed-up appearance, rather like a sick galah.

"Hullo, Mum." Approaching the chair, Mrs Capsella

greeted her mother nervously. I waited for the reply Pearly always gave her daughter on such occasions: "Hullo, stranger," but it didn't come.

"Mum's a bit under the weather," Neddy informed us cheerfully. "She's not used to travelling; the trip shook her up quite a bit."

Mrs Capsella patted at the woolly cardigan. "Can I get you something, Mum? Do you have a headache? Would you like an aspirin?"

"I've already had one," croaked Pearly. "Much good it's done me."

"Do you think you can get downstairs to the car? Or —"

"They'll have stretchers in the First Aid room," I volunteered. "We could get one of those."

Pearly's wrinkly lizard lids shot open and the gimlet eyes, fiercely blue, glared out at me. "Stretcher? What's he talking about? I'm not going on any stretcher, not while I've got the use of my own two legs." She rose huffily from her chair, smoothing her pink ruffled feathers, tweaking at her neat grey skirt. "Just give your father a hand with the luggage, will you, Ellen?"

"I'll do it." There wasn't much luggage at all, just a couple of old brown suitcases, real museum pieces, each with a single ancient label glued to its lid: *Fairy Falls Guest House, Katoomba*. Something told me this was where the Blounts had spent their honeymoon.

"So this is Melbourne," exclaimed Neddy as we emerged into the car park. He gazed up Collins Street, taking in the trams and the tall buildings and some tacky old bunting left over from last Christmas, or possibly the Christmas before that. "Look, Pearly!" he cried. "A real skyscraper."

"I'm not deaf, Neddy. And I've seen tall buildings before." Pearly's eyes slid nervously round the car park. "Where's Joe?" My father's name was Colin, but the Blounts always referred to him as Joe, after Joseph Stalin.

"Colin's away," said Mrs Capsella stiffly. "He had to go to a conference in Tasmania."

"Conference, eh?" whooped Neddy. "Mapping out the new Five Year Plan, are they?"

"It's a history conference, Dad. And I've told you before, Colin isn't —"

Pearly interrupted her. "If Joe's not here, then who's driving the car?" She glared at me suspiciously. "It's not *Al*, is it? If he's driving, then I'm —"

"It's all right, Mum. Al doesn't have a licence."

"*That* wouldn't stop him."

Mrs Capsella rattled her keys in a businesslike manner. "I'm driving."

"*What?*" Pearly clutched at Neddy's arm, "I'm not getting in that car if she's driving, Neddy, and that's a fact."

"Mum, it's all right. I can drive just as well as Joe, I mean, Colin. You'll be perfectly safe in my hands, won't she, Al?"

"Um, sure."

"Call a taxi, Neddy!"

"Now listen, Mum —"

Neddy took Mrs Capsella aside. "Best to humour her, Ellen," he whispered tactfully.

"But she always treats me like a *child!* Anyone would think I was twelve, the way she goes on!"

"Like I told you, she's a little bit under the weather. First the flood, and leaving Harris Park; you know how your mother is about that kind of thing." He sighed. "And then we had to get poor little Fluff put away."

"Fluff the dog? You mean he drowned?"

Mrs Capsella and I had given Fluff to Pearly after we'd stayed at Harris Park during the school holidays one year. He'd been scarcely bigger than a kitten when we found him at the pet-shop, with fluffy white hair and little blue eyes. The dog was just right for Pearly Blount. He belonged to her, the fluffiness and the glittering eyes and the bright pink tongue, the same shade as her fluffy woollies.

"No, no. No one drowned, Ellen. I meant we had to put him in a kennel for the duration. Mum was upset about that, and then there was a bit of an accident on the train, a small mishap with the folding sink. She's all shook up, best we don't aggravate matters. Best we get a taxi."

"I'll go with them, Mum," I offered. "Give me the key, so we can get into the house."

"But you can't all go off and leave me here!"

"You've got the car, Mum."

"But how will I find my way back through all those one-way streets? How can I look in the street directory while I'm driving?"

"Just take the right turns like everyone else and you won't need the directory. Go on the freeway, it's a straight trip, you'll be home before us."

"The freeway!" Mrs Capsella blenched.

"See, I told you," hissed Pearly. "We'd have been signing our death warrants, getting in there with her. The very idea! *Taxi!*" she bawled.

As the cab cruised smoothly towards the car park gates I thrust my head out of the window. "Brake on the left side!" I screeched. "Accelerator on the right!" Beside me, Pearly Blount let out her breath in a long-drawn hiss.

20

All in the Mind

Neddy Blount settled easily into our household. In no time at all he'd established the kind of routine he followed in his own home: in the mornings and early evenings he took a little walk about the neighbourhood, the rest of the day he spent in the garden, putting into action those rubbish disposal systems I'd attempted to describe to Ms Rock. The Blounts' garden in Harris Park consisted of a neat square lawn and a dazzling white path, bordered by weedless flower-beds and small blameless bushes clipped back to within an inch of their life. Our garden was very different: a jungly wasteland brimming with weeds and unkempt shrubs. Neddy had plenty of scope there. It must have seemed like Paradise to him; he was like a wasp let loose in a Mothers' Union cake stall. He snipped and pruned all day, and down in the garden shed, two shelves had been cleared of rusty paint cans, and now hosted a row of small newspaper packages.

But Pearly didn't adjust so easily. She took to her bed that first day, lying down beneath the covers, only her small pointed nose and wrinkly lizard lids showing above the sheets.

"She didn't even bother to put in her curlers last night," Neddy whispered. "She's never gone to bed without her curlers before." He kept padding into the room on tiptoe, bringing cups of tea and bread-and-butter plates of Iced Vovo biscuits. Pearly wouldn't touch them.

"Those biscuits might be stale," I suggested. "Mr Glix's stuff is pretty old."

Neddy bit into one, showering coconut down his front. "Fresh as a daisy," he pronounced.

"Enjoying yourself, are you?" Pearly remarked bitterly. Neddy passed her the plate again. "No, *thank* you. Out in the garden, I meant. Happy as Larry, aren't you, digging and snipping all day?"

"I wouldn't say that, exactly, Pearly," Neddy replied guiltily, but she only sniffed and turned her head away.

"Would you like me to read you something?" he offered, glancing at the bedside table where Pearly's small pleasures were laid out in a row: cigarettes and a box of Arctic mints, and two or three paperback novels, the kind Mrs Capsella wrote. "Would you like a chapter of *Nurse Sweetly Takes the Plunge*?"

Pearly sniffed again. "Go back to your garden," she replied huffily.

"Go in and say a few words to your grandmother," Mrs Capsella urged me when I came in from school next day. "See if you can cheer her up."

"She doesn't like me, she thinks I'm a lout."

"For heaven's sake, don't be so sensitive!" She gave me a small push towards the door. "Knock first," she instructed. "Don't just barge in."

Pearly was hunched beneath the eiderdown, a slit of fierce blue showing snakily beneath the lizard lids.

"Hi, Gran," I began uneasily.

The lids flicked open, the blue eyes sparked with irritation. "Don't call me 'Gran'," she hissed.

"Sorry." But what could I call her? She obviously

132

wouldn't approve of a kid addressing her by her first name. "Mrs Blount"? I stared at the small form on the bed. You had to feel sorry for her: she'd lived in that little house in Horatio Street for fifty years, and her life there was so orderly that whenever I thought of her, over a thousand kilometres away, I could picture exactly what she was doing. If it was ten o'clock on a Tuesday morning she'd be ironing the weekly wash, if it was a Thursday morning she'd be down at Slasher Joe's Discount Store, getting in the weekly shopping, and on any afternoon, from two o'clock till four, she'd be sitting in the small enclosed front verandah, knitting woollies and reading one of her nursie novels. Now all of this had gone, and Pearly was in a strange city, an unfamiliar house, lying in a bed which had a doona instead of a quilted satin spread, and up there on the wall, glowering down at her, was this big poster of a Heavy Metal group which I'd forgotten to remove. She must have felt weird, displaced, cast out, the way Lou and I did when we walked on past Never Never Land and then caught sight of our full-grown reflections in the window of the hardware store. Given the circumstances, even an ordinary old person might feel shaky, and Pearly was by no means ordinary.

And then, she had agoraphobia. I'd once seen a TV program on phobias; you cured them by gradually exposing the sufferer to the object or situation he was afraid of: spiders or toads or escalators or open spaces. But the point was, the process had to be gradual; you couldn't cure agoraphobia by hurling the sufferer over a thousand kilometres in a long-distance train; that was like chucking a handful of frogs at a person who shivered all over when he saw a tray of chocolate Freddos on the counter of a sweetshop. No wonder Pearly was freaking out.

133

I approached the bed softly. They say the first step, with a phobic subject, is to encourage them to talk about their fears. "You must feel a bit strange here," I began.

Pearly opened her eyes again, and stared, impassively, at the Heavy Metal poster.

"Really weird," I continued. "Being in a totally different place, all at once; it must be, well — unsettling."

The doona twitched slightly.

"I've got this friend, James, he's called, and he's got this — well, he hasn't really got it, he just thinks he has — this disease, called agoraphobia. He got it from studying for HSC, sitting round reading books all day and worrying. Never going out —"

Pearly's head turned slightly on the pillow. "Reading stunts your growth," she intoned.

"He's six foot four."

"Weedy though, is he? He'll be a skinny boy. No flesh on him, I'll be bound."

"He is a bit thin, but then he's always been like that. The thing is, Granny, I mean Pearly, I mean, uh — the thing about agoraphobia is that it's all in the mind, you see, it's only in your head. You don't really feel afraid of going out, or of new places, you just *think* you do. Once you actually get out, once you" — I glanced at the book on the bedside table — "take the *plunge* —"

Pearly sat up straight and glared at me. "Are you referring to *me*? Now listen here, young man —"

A sudden dismal thumping echoed through the house. Pearly flinched "What's that noise?"

"It's just the washing machine."

"Washing machine?" Pearly flung back the doona. "But it's Tuesday! Tuesday afternoon!"

"Yes, I know. You've been in bed for nearly two

whole days. But like I said, with agoraphobia, with any kind of fear —"

Pearly's eyes flashed sparks again. "Out!" she said.

"What?"

"Get out. I want to get dressed."

"Oh, sure thing. No worries, Grandma."

"And close the door!"

A few minutes later I heard her in the laundry talking to Mrs Capsella. "That big-mouthed son of yours told me I was a shingle short!"

"Oh surely not, Mum. You must have misunderstood him."

Pearly snorted. "Now *you're* doing it! There's nothing wrong with me, Ellen; I may be getting on a bit, but I've still got the use of all my faculties. No, that lout had the hide to come into my room and suggest that I was weak in the head. That I had some kind of mental disease called agoraphobia."

Mrs Capsella drew in her breath sharply. "I'm sorry about that, Mum. It's just this course he's doing at school, a kind of amateur psychology. He was suggesting something of the kind to Colin and me the other night. Just because we don't go to parties every weekend, he thinks —"

Pearly interrupted her. "And what do you think you're doing?"

"Doing? The washing, of course."

"But it's Tuesday!"

"So?"

"Monday is washing day, Ellen."

Mrs Capsella sighed irritably. "Not round here it isn't."

"And — and it's four o'clock in the afternoon. It's the *afternoon*, Ellen, people don't wash in the afternoon."

Mrs Capsella was silent.

"And what's this, what are you doing *there?* You don't put coloureds in with whites! And is that a *silk* shirt you're dumping in? Are you mad?"

"I *think* I've got the use of all *my* faculties," replied Mrs Capsella stiffly.

"It'll be ruined in the machine. Here, give it to me, silk has to be done by hand."

"No, leave it, I'll —"

"Give it here!"

There was a sharp ripping sound.

"Now look what you've done! You always were a stubborn child."

"Stubborn? If you'd left it where it was it would still be in one piece."

"Washing needs to be sorted, Ellen. First you do the coloureds, then the whites, then the delicates."

"That would take all day, Mum. As if I'm going to spend a whole day washing, I've more important things to do with my time."

"What can be more important than a good clean wash? In my day, we were up at crack of dawn, chopping kindling, stoking the copper, getting the water to a good fast boil."

The picture of the woman with the copper stick in our Human Development textbook flashed into my mind. Pearly obviously had pioneering blood in her veins.

I hurried into the garden; some instinct told me it was safer outside the house. "Pearly's up," I told Neddy.

"That's good news! I knew she'd be up and about soon, you can't keep a good woman down. Now" — he turned to the plot he was busily digging. "You've got quite a bit of oxalis here, Bertie. Once you get oxalis you've got to act fast."

I'd better explain that the Blounts always called me

"Bertie"; they thought that my real name was Albert. No one at school knows my real name — I try to keep it a secret. I've been "Al" for so long now that it's almost been forgotten. (Okay, it's "Almeric" — I can hardly bear to write it down; the Capsellas found the name in *Coles Funny Picture Book*. It means "Work Ruler" — can you imagine trying to live that down!) They didn't seem to have told the Blounts about "Almeric", however. I rather liked "Bertie", I regretted that I hadn't thought of it myself, years back.

Neddy handed me a fork, and for the next half-hour we weeded companionably, while from the house there echoed sounds of fretful bickering and the uncertain clatter of the washing machine labouring through an unfamiliar cycle. A door, which I guessed to be Mrs Capsella's, slammed abruptly, and a creaky old voice, Pearly's for sure, rose triumphantly in a snatch of old-fashioned song.

21

Under-age

Pearly waited for me when I came home from school. She didn't pretend, like Mrs Capsella used to do back in the days of her own sentry duty, that she was really doing something else, plucking the odd weed or watching for the mailman. Pearly had no hang-ups about being an anxious grandmother; like Broadside Williams, she was immune to embarrassment or guilt.

"You're late," she rasped.

I looked at my watch. It seemed to me that I was remarkably early; school had let out only a half-hour back and Sophie hadn't been waiting for me.

Every day as I left the shelter of the Year Eleven block I peered out over the playground, and every day now it was the same — nothing. The courtyards were empty, the oval deserted except for a few of King Arthur's detainees disconsolately picking up litter. The small waiting figure of Sophie had once made me nervous, but now she wasn't there I felt a flicker of some new kind of panic; a sense of being left behind, as if I was standing on an empty platform watching the lights of the train vanishing down the line. It mightn't have been the train I wanted to catch, but any train was better than waiting alone beside the empty tracks, uncertain when the next one might be coming, or even if there'd be another one at all.

"It's just four o'clock," I told Pearly. "School doesn't get out till three thirty."

"It's only a ten-minute walk from that place," she replied, primping her lips together in a tiny fan of smoker's pleats. "You've been dallying."

It was true I'd met up with Oz Padkin on the way home, but the whole conversation had taken less than ten minutes. I'd come across him in the dismal alley behind Glix's milk-bar. Oz was a writer now, not the type Mrs Slewt raved on about in English, but the kind who wrote on walls with cans of spray-paint. He had a can in his hand now.

"You want to lay off," I warned him. "Or change your style. All that poetry you're spraying everywhere, it's too easy to trace; you're the only kid in Laburnum who knows bits of Shakespeare by heart. If the cops go down to the school Mrs Slewt is going to dob you in. I heard her telling Ms Rock how she thought you'd degenerated."

Oz beamed. "Did she actually say I was a degenerate?"

"No. Just that you'd kind of — sunk. You're not exactly teacher's pet anymore, you know."

"What's the problem? What kind of nerd wants to be a teacher's pet when he's fourt— I mean, sixteen. Watch this!" He levelled a can at the high galvanised-iron fence which bounded Glix's back yard. "No Shakespeare this time!" I had to give it to him; he had talent all right. The letters, one metre high, appeared as if by magic. "HAPPY BIRTHDAY ON A TUESDAY!" they said.

"Hey! Glix'll have you for that!"

"Why should he? Free advertising, isn't it? If he paid

some professional to do this he'd be up for five hundred bucks at least."

"Look — if you don't pack it in you really *will* get a visit from the cops."

His eyes glowed with delight behind his thick glasses. "Really? Does that mean I'll actually have a record? Like a real Bogan? Like Tatts Logan? Hey — that rhymes! Listen —

'There once was a Bogan,
His name was Tatts Logan,
He —' "

"Listen, Oz, you've lived a pretty sheltered life up till now. A police record might sound exciting to you, but —"

"Sorry Al, I can't hang around for the rest of the sermon, I've got this — this date." He grinned. "Have to help someone with her homework. Seeya!" He belted off down the alley, can-laden pockets clanking against his knees.

"You've been hanging about with those friends of yours," accused Pearly. "Up to no good, I'll be bound." Her gimlet eyes peered at me from behind pink-rimmed glasses. I'd looked up the word "gimlet" in Mr Capsella's *Oxford Dictionary:* "a kind of boring-tool" it said.

"Where's Mum?" I asked.

The boring-tool smiled grimly. "Your mother's inside, cleaning out the linen press."

"Linen press? What's that?"

Pearly sucked in her breath sharply. "A linen press," she said slowly, enunciating each word carefully the way the teachers did when they were explaining some little matter to Cherry Clagg, "is a cupboard where you keep linen."

"Linen?"

"Sheets and towels, tablecloths, face-washers. And

that cupboard in the hall, that's your linen press." She shook her head. "Not that you'd know, with the higgle-piggle she's got in there."

I hurried inside. That linen press, as Pearly called it, was Mrs Capsella's storehouse of memories, the place where she kept all her old 'sixties gear. And there she was, standing knee-deep in embroidered jeans and mini skirts and lumpy clog-like shoes which bordered on the orthopaedic. "I've got to get out of here!" she gasped. "I can't stand it a moment longer. There's no privacy, no *respect!* It's like some terrible nightmare!" She took a few tottery steps towards me. "Have you ever had those nightmares where you're a teenager again, and your parents are hanging over you, dogging your footsteps, watching every move, listening in when you're on the telephone?"

"I *am* a teenager, Mum."

She stared at me blankly. "Oh yes, I forgot."

It was frightening. If Mrs Capsella imagined she was a teenager, what did that make me?

"Look, I'm going round to Dasher's for the evening."

"What? I'm coming too!"

"No you're *not*. Your grandparents are our guests, we can't all rush off and leave them here alone, it isn't nice. Besides, she'll snoop in my drawers and read my letters. You'll have to stay."

"Must I? They're *your* parents."

"You're staying, and that's that!" It was useless to argue, Mrs Capsella had slipped beyond the bounds of reason.

"Pearly's not going to like you buzzing off," I said slyly. "You know she doesn't approve of people going out."

"I've fixed all that. I've closed the door of my study

141

and left the light on, so it looks as if I'm in there, work-ing, get it?''

"Sure." It was a ruse I'd often employed myself.

"You just tell her I mustn't be disturbed."

"I don't think she'll take any notice of me. And how are you going to get out of the house?"

"I'll use the back window."

Good old Pearly caught her just a few feet from the gate. "Where are you going, Ellen?"

"Oh, there you are, Mum. I thought you were inside. Actually, I'm just going out."

"Going out?" Pearly was astonished. "How can you go out when it's nearly tea time?"

"No worries, Mum."

"No worries? What does that mean?"

"It's just an expression the kids use."

"You're hardly a kid, Ellen. What about the evening meal?"

"There's a casserole in the oven. And Al makes a lovely tossed salad."

"Salad? It's winter time, Ellen. You don't have salads in winter."

Mrs Capsella ground her teeth. "Then Al can boil some peas. He did Home Economics in Year Eight."

"You shouldn't make boys do kitchen work, Ellen. If the neighbours hear about it, they could get in the Child Welfare."

"I'm not going to argue, Mum. I'm a grown woman. I've got a perfect right to out when I want to."

Pearly changed tack. "Where are you going?"

"To a friend's place."

"Is this friend a lady?"

I snorted, thinking of Dasher's fishnet stockings and

long dangly earrings. Mrs Capsella shot me a furious glance. "Yes, she's a lady."

"What's her name?"

"Dasher."

"Dasher? Dasher?"

"Yes, *Dasher.*"

"Is this — person — married?"

Mrs Capsella hesitated. "Yes," I lied. I knew there was no way Pearly would allow her daughter to visit the home of a separated woman. "She's got a husband called Casper," I added.

Pearly tapped her foot. "Do you *have* to go there, Ellen, at this time of night?"

"For heaven's sake, Mum, it's only four thirty. It's not even dark yet. Actually," she went on shiftily, "it's a bit of an emergency. Her husband's got a very bad cold and I have to pick up a prescription for him at the chemist's. Dasher doesn't like to leave him."

Pearly hesitated. "I suppose if it's a question of illness —" She trailed up the driveway after her daughter, dogging her footsteps. "What time will you be back, then?"

"I'm not sure."

"Eight o'clock?"

"What? Oh no, later than that."

"How much later? Eight-thirty? Nine o'clock?" I listened in wonder. What a Watchdog! The condition was definitely hereditary.

Mrs Capsella shook herself all over, like a shaggy dog emerging from a cold bath. "Look Mum, I don't know exactly."

"Let's make it nine, then. Nine o'clock, no later, and if you're going to be later, if something unexpected happens, don't forget to give me a ring."

Silently, Mrs Capsella got into the car and began pedalling.

"Right pedal, Mum, *right!*"

The engine sputtered into life. "Nine o'clock!" bawled Pearly as the car disappeared down the road. She turned to me. "She'll kill herself in that thing!"

"Hey!" Neddy was beckoning to us from the bottom of the garden. "Come and get a gander at this, Bertie!" He waved an arm out towards the reserve.

"What is it, Grandpa?"

He shook his head, grinning. "A sweet sight, if ever I saw one."

"Shhh!" I warned, sure, from the soppy expression on his face, that he'd glimpsed Tatts Logan out there, taking the kiddies for a stroll. A sweet sight! Tatts would duff him up properly if he heard a remark like that. Neddy's age wouldn't protect him, Tatts had no qualms about assaulting the elderly. I gazed out over the fence. Drifting along the jogging track, hand-in-hand, were a boy and a girl, swinging their linked arms like best friends in kindergarten, pausing every few steps to gaze deeply into one another's eyes. It was Oz and Sophie! So that was why she hadn't rung lately, why she no longer waited for me in the playground after school! Again I had that lonely feeling of being left behind on the empty platform, the lights of the missed train winking down the track. I watched while Oz, on tiptoe, nuzzled at Sophie's neck.

Behind me Pearly clicked her tongue. "Silly girl," she muttered. "There's one born every minute."

"He's under-age," I muttered furiously.

"What?"

"That kid, that boy. He's only fourteen, he's under the age of consent."

144

"Consent for what, Bertie?" asked Neddy curiously, but I didn't wise him up, not with Pearly standing there.

She turned to me suddenly, a puzzled look in her eyes. "What kind of parents would call their girl Dasher?" she asked wonderingly. "It's a reindeer's name."

22

Old Wives' Tales

Every day, without fail, Pearly Blount rang Beryl's Bow Wowery, the select establishment where her little dog Fluff was boarded out. She wanted to check that he'd settled in properly and wasn't pining or fretting in his new quarters.

"It's a flash place, Bertie," Neddy confided, with a tinge of awe in his voice. "Heated kennels, three-course meals, hydro-bathing. They even have piped music."

"Sounds great," I said. "I wish we could go to a place like that for our holidays. You should see these filthy bush shacks Mum and Dad —"

"If you want to be boarded out in a kennel, Al, just let me know by November," said Mrs Capsella nastily. "Just so that I've got plenty of time to book you a room. Or would one call it a run? You won't need much luggage, just a collar and a rug, though I'm afraid you won't be able to take your ghetto blaster, it might set the neighbours howling."

Neddy seemed startled. "Bertie wouldn't want to stay in a kennel, Ellen," he protested mildly.

"Oh Dad, as if I really meant it!" Mrs Capsella sighed wearily: she and her parents were on such totally different wavelengths that communication was virtually impossible.

Pearly's phone calls always took place at six thirty in the morning. "Why do they have to ring at dawn?" groaned Mrs Capsella, who was by no means an early riser.

"Because that's when the dogs get up for breakfast, and that lady too, the person who runs it; Beryl Treetops."

"Beryl *Treetops!*"

The one thing Pearly had in common with her daughter, besides the watchdog syndrome, was a very loud, ringing voice. Her early morning conversation with Beryl Treetops could be heard all over the house. Beryl had good vocal organs too; I'd picked up the extension once, and her voice had rung out over the line; it was high and yappy, like a Pomeranian who'd cleverly learned to talk.

"Fluff is blooming, Mrs Blount," she barked. "Simply blooming. His coat is a wonder, and you'd be amazed at his appetite."

"Fluff is blooming, Neddy," Pearly carolled from the kitchen.

"Well!" Neddy clattered up the hall in his heavy old lace-ups and burst through my door; he'd obviously never heard of teenage privacy, and if I'd explained it to him he would have been deeply puzzled. "Fluff is blooming, Bertie," he boomed.

"That's great, Grandad. Great."

Neddy lumbered on into Mrs Capsella's room. "Fluff is blooming, Ellen."

Mrs Capsella's reply was muffled. A few minutes later she appeared in my doorway. "How long do houses take to dry out?" she whimpered. "It's been ten whole days. I can't take much more of this early rising."

"At least they go to bed early, nine o'clock on the dot."

"Yes, but they make *us* go to bed early, too. How much longer do you think they'll stay?"

I shrugged. "Why don't you ask them?"

"I can't do that! It would sound as if I was trying to get rid of them, and they're my parents, my only relatives."

"They mightn't be."

"What do you mean by that?"

"After you had that row with Pearly yesterday about ironing the tea-towels, she came and told me how when you were a baby she thought they might have made a mistake at the hospital. She said she asked for an exchange but they wouldn't take any notice of her."

"She *always* says that!" Mrs Capsella wailed. "She said it all the time when I was a teenager, imagine saying that kind of thing to your own child!"

The phone shrilled.

"Who can that be?" worried Mrs Capsella. "We don't know anyone who gets up at six. I hope nothing's happened to your father."

"It's Fluff!" Pearly cried. "It's Fluff. He's jumped the fence! Answer it, Neddy, I don't think I can, I feel weak as water."

"It's for you, Bertie," Neddy called. "Not Fluff at all. I'll just go and make Pearly a cup of tea, she's a bit shook up."

I picked up the receiver and heard James's gloomy voice on the line. "How many hours to countdown?" I asked cruelly.

"I just rang to tell you I'm heading off," he announced.

"Jumping the fence, are you?"

"What?"

"Nothing. Where are you heading off to? Been accepted into Mormon school?"

"Nah — those wankers wanted me to do a five-year course! I'm off to the bush. I'll camp out, catch a few bunnies, live off the land."

"I don't think you can do that any more. The bush is full of holiday houses; you'd be living in someone's back yard."

"You're just jealous," he growled, hanging up on me. I'd only got halfway across the room when he rang again. "Mum's running away!" he gasped, sounding scared. "I told her I was heading off, and then she chucked a mental and said *she* was running away. She means it, too — she's got her nursing qualification and that'll get her a job anywhere."

"She *mightn't* mean it."

"Yes she does! She's packing! Get your mum!"

"What?"

"Get your mum on the phone to talk her out of it! Dad's away in Adelaide on a business trip."

"Do you really think —"

"Just get her!"

I summoned Mrs Capsella to the phone, and wandered into the kitchen to drink tea with the Blounts. "What was all that about?" asked Pearly curiously. I tried to explain James's problem, but they didn't understand at all.

"You mean he's taking off just because of a bit of schoolwork?" Neddy was incredulous.

"It's not exactly 'a bit of schoolwork', Grandad. It's HSC — high stress, you know."

Neddy didn't know. "Funny thing to jump the fence about," he rumbled.

"Boy's got a screw loose," put in Pearly. "I knew it the moment I set eyes on him."

"Is he the funny-looking one?" asked Neddy.

Pearly shook her head. "The funny-looking one's

called Lou. This one is the long streak of misery who was round here the night before last." She turned to me. "Am I right?"

"Well, yes."

"Complaining about some disease he thought he had. Aph, aphids — only he's wrong there, aphids isn't a disease, not a human disease, it's an insect, you find them on rose bushes."

"If he's got aphids," chuckled Neddy. "He could fix himself up with a squirt of good old DDT."

"It's aphasia, not aphids," I said frostily. "It means you forget words."

"Forget words!" exclaimed Pearly. "As if any normal person forgets words. There's nothing the matter with that boy, except that he's a shingle short. It's all a big fuss about nothing, he hasn't any grit, that boy. He should meet Edie Mackintosh, shouldn't he, Neddy?"

Neddy winced slightly.

"Why," Pearly went on, "Edie's got things wrong with her the doctors never heard of, but she never lets it get her down. She's almost completely artificial: plastic knee, plastic heart valve, plastic hip, plastic —"

"More spare parts than an FC Holden," said Neddy.

"She should be in the *Guinness Book of Records*," said Pearly proudly. "And I've never once heard her complain — not since 1937, when her Ronnie went off with the cinema organist from the Roxy. She was well rid of that one."

Mrs Capsella strolled into the kitchen.

"Is Mrs Cadigorn still running away?" I asked.

"Not just yet. She's decided to do a Course instead."

"Course? You mean the one Mrs Padkin did, on teenage parenting?"

"No, this is another one, it's called 'Coping With HSC Stress'."

"Does she have to do assignments?" If Mrs Cadigorn got a lot of homework, I thought, then James would soon be ringing to say that Mr Cadigorn was running away.

"How should I know?" She gazed at me consideringly. "I hope I don't have to do a Course next year."

Pearly looked up from her cup of Tynee Tips. "You mean to tell me that a full-grown woman is going to do a Course, do *schoolwork?*" she gasped.

The series of early morning wake-up calls must have undermined Mrs Capsella's equilibrium. She flared up like a roman candle on cracker night. "I wish you wouldn't be so anti-intellectual, Mum," she cried. "You're a bad influence on Al. He's doing HSC himself next year and I've been trying to encourage him to do a bit more reading."

"Reading stunts your growth," said Pearly smugly.

"See? That's exactly what I mean! Of all the old wives' tales!"

"Old wives' tale, eh?" cackled Pearly. "You're a one to talk! Crouched over your books all day, and look at you now, hardly bigger than a twelve-year-old."

"I'm five foot three, Mum. And what about *you?* You're only four foot eleven!"

"Stuck in her room all day, wasn't she, Neddy? I told her and told her, 'reading stunts your growth,' I said, 'it ruins your eyesight, you'll be half-blind before you're forty.' She wouldn't listen, now look at her. Can't see a yard without those contact things. You'll be totally blind before you're fifty, my girl, mark my words!"

"You wear glasses, Mum!"

"Yes, but that's —"

"Now, then girls," said Neddy peaceably.

I left them to it. There was still an hour to go before school and I went back to my room and took out an

English novel from my schoolbag; suddenly I felt like doing a spot of reading.

The novel was all right, but the history book I opened later was really dull. Ms Rock was probably right, it might be a good idea to study with someone else, some serious-minded girl. Not Sophie, Oz was coaching her, perhaps someone like Kelly Krake. I reached for the phone; it was eight fifteen, she'd be getting ready for school, and it was better to talk on the phone than in the playground, with everyone listening in and drawing the wrong conclusions.

"Great," said Kelly. "Come round on Friday."

"Macca's having another party on Friday," I reminded her.

"Oh, yes." She paused.

"We could go together," I blurted out. "Save the study till another time, Sunday afternoon."

That was how you did things, I thought. Quickly, before you had time to brood about them, and imagine the consequences. Feeling suddenly decisive, I thought now might be the time to inform Mrs Capsella of my career plans.

She was in her room, sitting in front of some blank sheets of paper.

"Look at this!" she exclaimed irritably. "I've just been counting how many words I've managed to write since they arrived. Do you know what they add up to?"

I shook my head.

"Thirty-five! That's less than one paragraph. Hardly more than a sentence!"

"James counts words," I said. "That's how he started going off, thinking he had things wrong with him, agoraphobia and aphasia. Writer's block, in your case."

"Don't say it!"

"You should have taken up a more healthy profession. Listen, Mum, I've been meaning to tell you — I'm thinking of becoming a gardener."

"A gardener!"

"Keep your shirt on; I don't mean one of those nerds who go round mowing lawns. I mean a proper one, a landscape designer. I could go to horticultural college."

"Horticultural college!"

"What's wrong with that?"

"Oh, nothing." She paused. "It's all *his* fault, isn't it?"

"Whose?"

"Neddy's. All this raking and digging and tying twigs up in little parcels."

"He hasn't said a thing Mum, honest."

"I didn't mean that, I meant that it's hereditary."

"Yeah. So is being a Watchdog. Pearly's the worst Watchdog I've ever seen; that's where you get it from."

Mrs Capsella flushed. "I'm not a *Watchdog*. And if you're worried about that kind of thing, you'd better start praying they go before Friday night."

"Friday night?"

"Aren't you going to a party?"

"You've been listening on the phone again!"

"Of course I haven't — it's just that you've got such a loud, ringing voice it's impossible not to hear every word you say. Anyway, I'm warning you, if you're not back from that party by ten o'clock, Pearly will be round to pick you up."

"She wouldn't!"

"Don't bet on it; she did it to me all the time. She'd come round to my friend's house on Dad's old bicycle and ask, 'Is Ellen here?'"

"Don't tell her where your bike is!"

Mrs Capsella shrugged. "That won't stop her. She'll

153

find some other means of transport; she might even let me give her a lift."

I stood rooted to the spot. Struck dumb, and it wasn't aphasia. It was Wednesday; there was no doubt about it, before Friday night, the Blounts had to go.

23

All Shook Up

"Pearly's really nuts about that little dog, isn't she?" remarked Lou thoughtfully.

"Sure. She's knitting him this tiny little coat, pink, with his name embroidered in blue."

"*Très chic,* but get your mind off the doggy fashions and concentrate for a moment. If Pearly thought he was fretting for her, she'd be off on the next train, wouldn't she? Even if the house wasn't ready and she had to pitch a tent outside the Bow Wowery. So — we ring up and pretend to be the dog."

"They're not *dumb*, idiot. Even Pearly doesn't think Fluff can talk on the telephone."

"You're the one who's dumb. I didn't mean the dog, I meant that lady who runs the joint, what's her name?"

"Beryl Treetops."

"Right!" he snorted. "So we ring up and pretend to be Beryl and we say the pup's freaked out, fretting and pining for Pearly, and if she doesn't get back right away he's liable to pop off."

I didn't say anything.

"Well," pressed Lou. "What do you think?"

"It's a bit cruel — Pearly would be really shook up."

"But isn't that what you want? If she gets shook up,

155

she'll go home, and anyway, what could be crueller than being picked up from a party by your grandmother?''

I hesitated.

"Look, if your mum's started counting words, that's a bad sign, isn't it? She might decide to become a Mormon, like James. Though actually James has improved since your granny had a few words with him.''

"When was that? What did she say?''

"I don't know exactly; she told him some weird stuff about a woman made out of plastic. And he hates the way she calls him 'a long streak of misery'.''

"Oh.''

"And that's another thing: if you don't get rid of her soon you won't have a friend left. I don't like going round to your joint myself; she's downright insulting.'' He paused, flushing slightly, as if at some painful memory. "So what about the phone call?''

"I suppose we could say that Fluff was fretting just a *little* bit.''

"Sure, if you like, if you think that's enough to get her moving.''

"It's enough. But what about when she rings up Bow Wowery the next morning?''

"The point is, if we time it right, there won't *be* a next morning. We'll ring up this evening, say, round six o'clock, and that will just give them time to pack up and catch the late train. We can use the phone outside Glix's milk-bar. I'll meet you there at six, right?''

"Right.''

It was dark when I reached the phone-box; the winter nights were closing in early. Lou was waiting impatiently, stamping his feet against the cold. His eyes gleamed with excitement, he liked this sort of thing, a bit of fun on a dull schoolday evening . . . and if the fun went wrong, no one was going to pin the blame on him. "Come on!" he urged.

We squeezed into the box. "I'll be Beryl Treetops," he said eagerly. "There's less of a risk that way, in case your mother answers the phone."

"Look, I'll do it. I can disguise my voice." To be frank, I didn't trust him; he was capable of anything, he was liable to get carried away and say the dog was dead. "Besides," I added, "I know what Beryl Treetops sounds like. She's got this voice like a Pomeranian."

"A Pomeranian?"

"High and yappy; it's hard to imitate if you haven't actually heard it."

"Okay, then I'll be the dog."

"We don't need the dog."

"Yes we do, for authenticity. You say, 'Hullo, is that Mrs Blount? I'm afraid I've got some *rather* sad news, little' — what's his name?"

"Fluff."

" 'Little Fluff is —' " he grinned — " 'just a teeny bit under the weather. I think he might be fretting —' And then I'll bark in this slow, sad sort of way, as if I'm very weak —"

Someone knocked on the door of the phone-box. "Just our luck," grumbled Lou. "Probably some old lady wants to ring an ambulance." He pushed the door open and stuck his head outside. There was a murmur of conversation, and an icy blast of cold air on my neck.

"Shut the door, will you? Who is it?"

"It's okay, just Oz and Sophie. I was explaining the situation to them, they're going to give us a hand."

"We don't need a hand. There's not enough room in here."

But Oz was already thrusting his way into the box, dragging Sophie behind him.

"Hullo," I said weakly, and she smiled at me distantly, as if I was some person whose name she couldn't quite recall.

"Bit of a squeeze," whispered Lou. "Lucky Kelly Krake isn't here, or we'd be squashed flat."

"Shut up!" I picked up the receiver, slotted in the coins and dialled our number.

"Just a minute!" Oz dashed the receiver from my hand, and the coins slid out on the tray.

"Watch what you're doing!"

"But you've got to have pips, Al. You're ringing from Sydney, remember; it's long distance. I'll do the pips."

I slid the coins back into the slot and dialled again. Mrs Capsella answered.

"Pip pip pip pip pip," squeaked Oswald.

"Hullo, could I talk to Mrs Pearly Blount, please? This is Beryl Treetops, of Beryl's Bow Wowery, speaking."

"Yap yap yap, *ooh*," bayed Lou.

"Not now, you idiot," I hissed.

"Is that you, Al?" cried Mrs Capsella. "Why are you calling yourself Beryl Treetops? And what's that awful howling sound?"

"It's just Lou, Mum."

"Is he sick? Is he having an asthma attack? Where are you?"

"Nothing's wrong, Mum. It's a joke. We're just up the road, in the phone-box."

"Come home at once, do you hear? Your grandmother's very upset."

"How could she be? I haven't even said anything about the dog yet."

"What dog? Stop mucking about and come home, I want a bit of support here. First your father runs off, and then you —"

The phone-box darkened suddenly. A huge shape loomed against the glass and there was a hammering on the door.

"What's that?" squeaked Mrs Capsella.

"Nothing, Mum, no worries." I slammed down the phone.

"It's Tatts Logan!" breathed Lou.

"Let's get out of here!" We bundled ourselves through the door.

"Just a minute! Not so fast!" Tatts caught hold of Lou's sweatshirt. "What were you doing in that box, Pine?"

"Nothing, Tatts. Just making a call."

"Don't give me that crap! You were barking, I heard you, barking at this girl here, making a little nuisance of yourself."

"Geez no, I wasn't, was I, Sophie?"

Tatts yanked at his shirt.

"He wasn't, Mr Logan," said Sophie. "He wasn't barking at me."

"We were just making a phone call to a friend," said Oz. "A joke call, if you know what I mean."

"You're not allowed to make hoax calls," said Tatts primly. "It's against the law; it's called Committing a Public Nuisance."

"You should know," I muttered.

"What's that, Capsella?" Tatts released his hold on Lou and grabbed me by the belt, lifting me off the pavement.

"Malcolm! Put that boy down at once, do you hear me?" Sharon Guppy appeared round the corner from the milk-bar, the twins scuttling along by her side.

"Daddy!" They flung themselves at their father's legs. Tatts' fingers went limp; I slid from his hands onto solid earth again.

"I've been waiting *hours* for that gripe-water, Malcolm," complained Sharon.

"Geez, Shar, it's not my fault. There was some old guy in the milk-bar telling Glix his life story. I had to wait."

"Well, you're not waiting now, are you? Just leave those boys alone and come home. The tea's on the table getting stone cold!"

Tatts trailed off after his little family. At the corner, he turned back to us. "It's a one thousand dollar fine for Committing A Public Nuisance," he hissed. "Now clear off or I'll report you to the cops!"

"Malcolm!"

"And that's the guy who demolished practically every phone box in Laburnum!" sighed Lou. "It's depressing."

It really was.

24

Ingratitude

I almost stumbled over Pearly's small figure in the darkened driveway. She was standing by the gate, dazed looking, wringing her tiny little hands and squinting anxiously up and down the street.

"Is something the matter, Grandma?"

She was so upset she didn't notice I'd used the forbidden term; I don't think she saw me at all.

Mrs Capsella was fretting on the terrace, pacing up and down beside Dasher's potplants and the two old brown suitcases.

"Are they *going?*"

"They were. A call came through to say the house was ready and Mum wanted to go off at once, tonight, so they wouldn't miss the Leagues Club dance tomorrow night."

"Does Pearly *dance?*" I knew they went to the Club on Saturday nights — it was their only outing — but I couldn't imagine my grandparents *dancing*.

Mrs Capsella ignored the question. "But now," she went on, "Dad's disappeared."

"Disappeared? How could he?"

"I don't know! He went out for one of his walks, around five o'clock, and he didn't come back."

"Think he's scarpered?"

"Don't be an idiot. And keep your voice down, she'll hear you!"

"I think she's back in shock."

Mrs Capsella ran a wild hand through her kelp-coloured hair. "Do you think I should ring the police?"

"Look, don't worry, I'll scout round the block; he's probably just lost his way in the dark."

We hurried down the driveway towards Pearly. Mrs Capsella tapped her on the shoulder. "Al's going to look for him, Mum," she said. "He thinks Dad's just lost his way in the dark."

Pearly peered at me doubtfully. "He's never lost his way yet," she moaned. "He *always* comes home on time. Now it's six thirty, and there's no sign of him!" Her voice rose to a wail. "It's this *place* — all this coming and going, to-ing and fro-ing, people going out whenever they feel like it and coming back at all hours! You've unsettled him! You always were an unsettling child, Ellen."

Halfway up the street, a movement caught my eye. Two dark shapes were moving slowly along beside the fences, one small, the other tall and slightly stooped; a cigarette glowed softly in the dark.

"He's coming now!" I yelled. "I can see him, he's just outside Lou's place."

As the two figures passed under the street-light, Mrs Capsella let out a little scream. "That man! That man with Dad! Look at him — he's tall, he's got big feet, he's *smoking* —"

"It's okay, Mum."

"It's the prowler!"

"Prowler," breathed Pearly hoarsely, "Is Neddy out walking with prowlers now?"

"No worries, Mum," I told Mrs Capsella. "I know that man."

"You *know* him? You know a prowler?"

"It's just Mr Disher, Sophie's dad."

"Just because he's the father of one of your friends doesn't make him all right, Al."

"He's harmless, really, Mum." I crossed my fingers; I wasn't quite sure about Mr Disher.

"But he was tapping on our window that night!"

"No, that was James, looking for me."

"There was a woman tapping on our window last night," Pearly broke in excitedly. "A woman in her nightie. She said she was looking for someone."

"You must have dreamed that, Mum."

"It was no dream, Ellen. It was real." Pearly raised her voice. "Neddy!" she called. "Come away from that man! Come home at once!"

Neddy sauntered down the footpath. Mr Disher, with a small wave in my direction, wandered off in the direction of the reserve, his cigarette burning sadly in the dark.

"You should be careful who you talk to, Grandad," I said. "There are some funny people about."

"He's a nice fellow," murmured Neddy, avoiding Pearly's stony gaze. "I had quite a yarn with him. You won't believe this, Pearly, but the poor chap has to walk the streets if he wants to take a smoke. They won't let him do it in the house!" He shook his head.

"You're late, Neddy," said Pearly, unmoved.

"And that chap at the milk-bar, Mr Glix, he's quite a character. Look what he had in stock! You wouldn't find this in a Harris Park milk-bar!" He drew an envelope from his pocket, slid out the card and handed it to me. "Happy Birthday on a Tuesday," I read.

"Your birthday's on a Tuesday, this year, isn't it, dear?" he said to Pearly. "Born on a Tuesday, too!"

He broke into verse:

"Monday's child is fair of face,
Tuesday's child is full of grace . . ."

The gracious one gave him a push which would have done justice to Tatts Logan. "Get the bags!" she ordered. "I want to catch that train and get back home again, I want to be inside my own house, where there's peace and quiet. I want to put my feet up and relax!" She turned to Mrs Capsella. "Call me a taxi, will you, Ellen."

"I can drive you, Mum."

Pearly stamped her foot. "Call me a taxi!"

Mrs Capsella strode huffily inside to the telephone.

Fifteen minutes later we stood at the gate making our farewells. Neddy leaned out of the taxi window. "We had a wonderful time, Ellen," he beamed, "Wonderful."

"Speak for yourself," scowled Pearly. She gazed scornfully at the darkened garden, the lighted house, the strange streets of Laburnum where her Neddy had almost disappeared. She turned accusingly on Mrs Capsella and me. "It was like — like living in the Twilight Zone," she hissed.

We watched the lights of the taxi vanishing down the road. "Ingratitude!" muttered Mrs Capsella.

"Well, I'll be off now, Mum. Seeya."

"Off? Where are you going?"

"Just up to Lou's for a bit."

"What time will you be back?"

I stared at her incredulously. After all we'd been through she hadn't learned a thing!

"Watchdog!" I growled.

GLOSSARY

Box of stubbies – small squat bottles of beer or the beer in them

Bughouse – Small plastic container to hold insects for observation

Chocolate Freddos – Frog-shaped chocolates, a favourite in school lunch-boxes

Daggy hole – Scruffy hang-out

Dag – Boring or uncool person

Dill – Twit

Dob James in – Inform on James

Doona – Duvet

Dragster – Souped-up car for drag racing

EC Holden and FC Holden – Australian-produced cars

Galah – Fool

Glory-box – Bottom drawer

Lamingtons – Square cakes rolled in coconut

Op shops – Shop selling secondhand clothes and knick-knacks

Show-bags – Carrier bags packed with samples of sweets, crisps

Smoker's pleats – Lines around a smoker's mouth

Stubbies – Cut-off jeans

Utility – Small pick-up truck

Other Books from
The O'Brien Press

MISSING SISTERS
Gregory Maguire

In the fire at the orphanage's holiday home, Alice's favourite nun is injured. Back at the orphanage, Alice is faced with difficult choices, then a surprise enters her life when she meets a girl called Miami.

Paperback £3.99

THE SECRET CITY
Carolyn Swift

When Nuala and Kevin visit the hidden city of Petra in the mysterious land of the Bedouin, they find themselves involved in intrigue and strange happenings.

Paperback £3.99

COULD THIS BE LOVE? I WONDERED
Marilyn Taylor

First love for Jackie is full of anxiety, hope, discovery. Kev *seems* interested in her, but what is he really thinking? And what should she do about Sinead?

Paperback £3.99

CHEROKEE
Creina Mansfield

Gene's grandfather Cherokee is a famous jazz musician and Gene travels the world with him. He loves the life and his only ambition is to be a musician too. But his aunt has other plans!

Paperback £3.99

THE HEROIC LIFE OF AL CAPSELLA
Judith Clarke

Al Capsella's parents are a constant embarrassment and definitely *not* normal. Desperate to be cool, Al devises all sorts of schemes for suviving their abnormal behaviour. Until he discovers that being really normal is the strangest thing of all.

Paperback £3.99

AMELIA
Siobhán Parkinson

Almost thirteen, Amelia Pim, daughter of a wealthy Dublin Quaker family, loves frocks and parties, but now she must learn how to live with poverty and the disgrace of a mother arrested for suffragette activity.

Paperback £3.99

NO PEACE FOR AMELIA
Siobhán Parkinson

Amelia's friend, Frederick, enlists for the Great War, whilst servant Mary Ann's brother is involved with the Easter Rising and wants her to hide him in the Pim home. The issues for Amelia are love and war.

Paperback £4.50

ON SILENT WINGS
Don Conroy

After his mother's death, a young barn owl is left alone to survive in a world he does not yet know. Who is the Emperor of Fericul who threatens him?

Paperback £4.99

THE CELESTIAL CHILD
Don Conroy

During a violent storm, a young girl sees a strange boy who seems to glow in the dark. He has remarkable powers. But who or what is this unusual person?

Paperback £4.99

THE CASTLE IN THE ATTIC
Elizabeth Winthrop

There is a strange legend attached to the model castle given to William by Mrs Phillips. William is drawn into the story when the silver knight who guards the castle comes to life.

Paperback £3.99

THE BATTLE FOR THE CASTLE
Elizabeth Winthrop

The sequel to *The Castle in the Attic*. William must use his wits to face an evil force intent on the total destruction of the world. As he battles to save the castle, William discovers that there is more than one way to become a hero.

Paperback £3.99

THE CHIEFTAIN'S DAUGHTER
Sam McBratney

A boy fostered with a remote Irish tribe 1500 years ago becomes involved in a local feud and with the fate of his beloved Frann, the chieftain's daughter.

Paperback £3.99

UNDER THE HAWTHORN TREE
Marita Conlon-McKenna

Eily, Michael and Peggy are left without parents when the Great Famine strikes. They set out on a long and dangerous journey to find the great-aunts their mother told them about in her stories.

Paperback £3.95

WILDFLOWER GIRL
Marita Conlon-McKenna

Peggy, from *Under the Hawthorn Tree*, is now thirteen and must leave Ireland for America. After a terrible journey on board ship, she arrives in Boston. What kind of life will she find there?

Hardback £6.95 Paperback £4.50

THE BLUE HORSE
Marita Conlon-McKenna

When their caravan burns down, Katie's family must move to live in a house on a new estate. But for Katie, this means trouble. Is she strong enough to deal with the new situation?

Paperback £3.99

NO GOODBYE
Marita Conlon-McKenna

When their mother suddenly leaves, the children and their father must cope. They experience frustration – and a few new thrills as well. But the real question is: Will she come back?

Paperback £3.99

THE HUNTER'S MOON
Orla Melling

Cousins Findabhair and Gwen defy an ancient law at Tara, and Findabhair is abducted. In a sequence of amazing happenings, Gwen tries to retrieve her cousin from the Otherworld.

Paperback £3.99

HOUSE OF THE DEAD
Michael Scott

When Patrick and Claire go on a school trip to Newgrange, they release a power that threatens the existence of the human race. They must defeat it, but what chance have two teenagers against the ancient magic?

Paperback £3.99

MOONLIGHT
Michael Carroll

The body of a 10,000 year-old horse is discovered and a genetic engineer and a ruthless businessman dream of the fastest racehorse ever. But can Cathy outwit them and protect the new-born foal?

Paperback £3.99

ORDER FORM

These books are available from your local bookseller. In case of difficulty order direct from THE O'BRIEN PRESS

Please send me the books as marked

I enclose cheque / postal order for £……… (+ 50p P&P per title)

OR please charge my credit card ☐ Access / Mastercard ☐ Visa

Card number ☐☐☐☐ ☐☐☐☐ ☐☐☐☐ ☐☐☐☐

EXPIRY DATE ☐ ☐ ☐ ☐

Name: …………………………………………Tel: ………………

Address: ……………………………………………………………

……………………………………………………………………

Please send orders to : THE O'BRIEN PRESS, 20 Victoria Road, Dublin 6.
Tel: (Dublin) 4923333 Fax: (Dublin) 4922777